## *"Sorry if I've kept*

What an apology. In the best of all possible worlds, Sam could keep her up all night. No complaints.

But this was the real world. With real limitations and consequences. And Julia had to go up to her bed.

*Alone.*

"Thanks for inviting me to stay."

She could barely think, barely breathe, with him standing so close to her.

"We never got a chance to talk about Lester and Lucy," she realized.

"Not get into another argument, you mean?" He lifted her chin with his fingertip, so that she was looking into his eyes again. And couldn't look away.

And didn't want to.

"I'd rather not argue with you, Julia. In fact, I think I'm done talking altogether."

Before Julia could say a word more, he pulled her close. She felt as if she didn't have a chance. Didn't have a choice…

Dear Reader,

Do you ever find yourself in a sticky situation and no matter how you try to fix things, your tactic always backfires and just makes things worse? That is more or less the story of Julia Martinelli, who you may remember from *Dad in Disguise,* the first of the BABY DAZE miniseries.

Rachel Reilly's best friend Julia had such a strong, vibrant personality, I knew she had to have her own romantic adventure. Add to that her charming but eccentric mother Lucy—The Merry Widow of Blue Lake, Vermont—and I had all the ingredients for a non-stop romantic comedy of errors.

The harder Julia tries to save her mother from a hasty marriage to appliance repairman Lester Baxter, the more confusion she causes for everyone. Including herself, as she falls head over heels for Sam Baxter, the gorgeous, charming, irresistible son of Lucy's husband-to-be.

Loving, loyal and overly responsible Julia has some lessons to learn. Mainly, about letting go of her own careful plans—and letting love conquer all.

I hope you enjoy *The Baby Plan* and all the books in the BABY DAZE series.

Wishing you happy reading—

*Kate Little*

# THE BABY PLAN

## KATE LITTLE

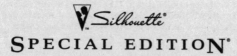

Silhouette®

SPECIAL EDITION®

Published by Silhouette Books

America's Publisher of Contemporary Romance

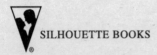

SILHOUETTE BOOKS

ISBN-13: 978-0-373-24900-8
ISBN-10:    0-373-24900-4

THE BABY PLAN

---

## KATE LITTLE

claims to have lots of experience with romance—"the *fictional* kind, that is," she is quick to clarify. She has been both an author and an editor of romance fiction for over fifteen years. She believes that a good romance novel will make the reader experience all the tension, thrills and agony of falling madly, deeply and wildly in love. She enjoys watching the characters in her books go crazy for each other, but she hates to see the blissful couple disappear when it's time for them to live happily ever after. In addition to writing romance novels, Kate also writes fiction and nonfiction for young adults. She lives on Long Island, New York, with her husband and daughter.

## *Chapter One*

Something was up.

Julia Martinelli had a funny feeling. She'd developed a sixth sense for these things by now. An uncanny radar for her mother's imminent romantic misadventures.

Her mother's invitation for dinner had sounded innocent enough. They lived in the same town, the place where Julia had been raised, and got together at least once a week for dinner or lunch, or just to say hello over coffee.

But for some inexplicable reason, Julia's skin went all shivery with goose bumps during this particular call. Something in her mother's tone signaled *Watch out. Something's cooking. It's not just Mom's special meat loaf.*

Julia didn't ask any questions. She didn't want to seem overly suspicious. Her mother had become very sensitive to any inquiries about her love life and Julia had to tiptoe around the subject these days, which wasn't easy. Her mother was a master at avoiding a straight answer.

"You're always imagining things, dear," Lucy Martinelli would claim. As if Julia was the one with the problem—or "issues" as folks on TV talk shows liked to say.

Julia knew she did have a few "issues" about romance: the greatest one being, she couldn't find much of it. Not the kind she was looking for. Her mother, on the other hand, found more than enough for anyone. Especially a woman her age. Which was often…a problem.

As Julia drove over to her mother's after work on Friday night, she was gripped by the same unnerving sensation, and the palms of her hands were clammy on the steering wheel. Was she only imagining things? She dearly hoped so.

In the small town of Blue Lake, Vermont, Julia's mother Lucy was known as "The Merry Widow"—though technically speaking, only two of Lucy's four husbands had died.

Marriages two and four had ended in divorce. Which did not bode well for husband Number Five, Julia thought, if and when he arrived. The odd-numbered husbands seemed to have a high mortality rate.

All things considered, it was more a matter of when than if. Julia just knew Number Five was out there somewhere, hovering on the horizon. A new chapter in her mother's relationship saga, which Julia often thought could provide more than enough material for some thick, juicy novel or a made-for-TV movie.

Married first to her high school sweetheart, Lucy became a widow at the tender age of twenty-one, when her young husband died in a boating accident. She next married Julia's father, Tom Martinelli, a local attorney. That union lasted over twenty years, though Julia knew now that her parents had stayed together mainly because of her, both feeling out of synch with their spouse, but committed to giving their only child a stable family life.

It wasn't an unhappy household, though even as a child Julia sensed something was missing between her parents. As a grown woman, she decided she'd never make that same choice—to stay stuck in a loveless relationship.

Her parents divorced while Julia was in college. Her father had since retired and moved to Florida with his second wife, Adele, a former elementary school teacher. They played a lot of golf and were ardent fans of the History Channel—pastimes that had never interested Julia's mother.

Julia loved her father dearly and knew she took after him more in temperament, but she was still objective enough to see her mom was definitely having more fun.

Shortly after the divorce, Lucy took a weekend jaunt to Las Vegas with some girlfriends. There she met and married a retired Texas businessman, fell head over heels and walked up the aisle that very weekend in the tackiest of Vegas wedding chapels.

Julia had not been present, but the blurry instant photos told the whole story. Earl T. Walker was a lovely man, but much older than Lucy. He died from a sudden heart attack a few weeks before the couple's third anniversary.

Lucy inherited a sizable portion of Earl's estate, but there was nothing left for her in Texas. She'd never taken well to the wide open spaces and Lucy soon returned to Blue Lake. She'd never sold her house there so it was easy to settle back into the community, her old routines and connections. She found plenty of sympathy from her friends and from Julia. But at least Lucy had found some years of happiness during her brief third marriage, unlike some people who never find anyone to love.

Encouraged by that success, Lucy's next husband, number four, appeared with jaw-dropping speed. He was clearly a rebound match, with Lucy falling for the agent who handled the life insurance claim on number three. Before anyone could say double indemnity, it was back to the divorce courts.

Now, here they were. Lucy had lasted several years in the single life, but remained undaunted in her quest to find true love. All things considered, it seemed only a matter of time before

Number Five arrived. Her mother was still attractive, in good health and rarely without a date on a Saturday night. She just had a knack for meeting men without even trying.

After all she'd been through, Lucy had never once spoken a single word against matrimony, or soured toward the institution in any way. After being twice widowed and twice divorced, she certainly had enough assets to live independently in fine style for the rest of her days. But marriage meant more to Lucy than financial security. Julia knew her mother's lace-trimmed valentine heart still yearned to find her perfect match, her "soul mate." She totally believed in the notion that such a man existed.

Julia didn't believe in soul mates. Or love at first sight, or any of those worn-out clichés, none of which could describe Lucy's romantic philosophy. Maybe she was too rational about male-female relationships. Someone in the family had to be.

Julia hadn't always been this way. Time and experience had worn down her romantic spirit and given her a more realistic view. Julia was actually a bit envious of her mother. Not of Lucy's addiction to walking down the aisle, but of her unflagging optimism. Julia was secretly starting to lose hope of ever finding Mr. Right. Or even Mr. Fixer-Upper.

Julia sometimes wondered if she really wanted a husband at all. Being perfectly honest with herself, she seemed to have reached the point when the only thing she really wanted was a baby.

As she slowly but surely approached her thirty-second birthday, the biological messages to make a baby were flashing like a warning system gone berserk. She'd just about given up taking the traditional route of romance and marriage.

Julia had only once admitted this aloud to her best pal, Rachel Reilly. Rachel was the perfect advisor on the subject, having faced the same dilemma a little over two years ago when her fiancé had left her at the altar. She'd decided not to wait for a man to give her the life she wanted and had taken a courageous leap, becoming a single mother by choice as a client of a sperm bank.

Julia admired Rachel's courage and decisiveness. She often wondered if she could ever do the same. As it turned out, Jack Sawyer, the sperm donor dad, eventually sought out Rachel and their little boy. Miraculously, Rachel and Jack eventually found their own happily ever after.

Julia knew their story was a heartwarming fluke. She knew if she took that route, she'd have to be prepared to do it all on her own.

Every time she considered it, the complications of living in a small town where people still clung dearly to traditional ideas about marriage and child-rearing seemed too big an obstacle. Julia was a successful Realtor with a high profile in the community. Having a baby on her own would stir up a storm of gossip. Living under the cloud of her mother's misadventures had been enough public attention. Julia knew for certain she didn't want the whole town talking about her, too.

Her livelihood would definitely suffer. Not that she was materialistic, but she had to think about supporting a child.

Mulling over all these familiar questions that never seemed to have answers, Julia drove through the village toward her mother's house. It was a clear winter night in late February. A fresh dusting of snow made the winding streets and quaint houses look cozy and inviting, like an illustration from a picture book.

Julia knew practically every house on every lane from attic to cellar. And she knew the people within, the previous owners and the ones before that. She loved living in Blue Lake and was a perfect town-booster to newcomers searching for a country retreat or locating out of the city. Which was just the way she and Rachel had first met and become fast friends.

Rachel teased her now about running for mayor. But Julia wasn't interested in politics. Besides, she knew the job wouldn't work with the role of motherhood any better than her present profession.

As much as she loved Blue Lake, these days she'd started to regret never taking her chance out in the wide world, where she could be anonymous and private, casting her line in a larger pool of slippery, hard-to-reel-in bachelors.

Maybe the same rule applied to finding a husband as finding a house. *Location. Location. Location.*

How had she ended up here all this time anyway? She'd always meant to leave. But she'd married a hometown boyfriend right after college and by the time they divorced, her business was firmly established. And it also seemed important by then to stick around to keep an eye on Lucy. As an only child, she felt even more responsible.

Attractive and charming, in a field where she met new people all the time, Julia never lacked invitations from eligible men… and even some that weren't so eligible. She joked to her friends that she'd dated every male possibility in a fifty-mile radius. But it wasn't really a joke and those relationships never seemed to lead anywhere.

All she really wanted was a mature, solid relationship. A meeting of the minds…and hearts. Someone she could respect and get along with. Someone who wanted the same things in life she did. Was that so much to ask?

There had to be a spark, of course. Chemistry. Attraction. Julia wasn't so practical-minded that she'd skip all those heady feelings. Still, being totally swept off her feet scared her, because she knew it could never last. Case in point—her mother. Lucy was always being swept off her feet. Struck by lightning. Head over heels on a first date, before the waiter had even taken her dinner order.

Did any of it last? Of course not.

Julia knew it took a lot for her to fall in love. She knew that her unhappy marriage and divorce made her wary. Sometimes she thought she was too particular. She couldn't help it. She wasn't going to get married again just to show the world and herself—and maybe even her mother—that she could.

Meanwhile, her mother was exactly the opposite, in and out

of relationships, dating and dumping or being dumped and moving on to the next partner. Her love life was a game of musical chairs and every time she landed, she was sure "This is it!"

Had her mother landed anywhere lately? Lucy hadn't mentioned dating anyone special that Julia could recall. But her mother was so chatty during their phone calls, Julia knew she may have missed some crucial information while multitasking.

Julia turned down Magnolia Way and pulled into the driveway at her mother's house. The depressing vision of herself at her mother's age, living alone, surrounded by cats, rose up to fill her mind. No matter that her mother didn't have any cats.

She pushed the image out of view. Her mother would doubtlessly ask about her social life tonight and Julia knew it was important to put a positive, upbeat face on the situation. When in fact, it was anything but.

Seven o'clock sharp, Julia stood at the front door, a box from the bakery in hand. A triple-layer chocolate cake laden with chocolate icing. Julia normally stayed away from such potent treats, but it was Lucy's favorite. Her mother was an unrepentant chocoholic, always had been, stashing candy bars around the house when Julia was growing up. She never knew where she might find them.

Julia had read somewhere that an ingredient in chocolate triggered the same hormonal fireworks in the brain that were set off when people fell in love. No wonder Lucy couldn't go a day without her Hershey's Kisses. If the little foil-wrapped version would keep her away from the real ones, Julia was all for it.

She knocked once and the door sprang open. As if Lucy had been standing in the foyer, waiting for her.

"There you are. Right on time. You're always so punctual, dear. You don't take after me that way."

It was a good thing, Julia thought. In more ways than one.

Lucy smiled, then raised herself on tiptoe to kiss Julia's cheek.

At five foot ten Julia was taller than most women, including her mother, who was stood at a petite five foot three. It had been awkward to be so tall when she was a teenager. Especially before any of the boys had caught up. By now, she'd learned to live with it. Even enjoy it. She had the slim build and long legs to pull it off with enviable elegance. When she entered a meeting room for a tough negotiation, it definitely helped to meet her adversaries—most of them male—eye-to-eye.

Lucy helped her off with her coat and hung it in the closet.

"Don't you look nice," Lucy said. "I love you in red. Bold colors suit you, Julia. Not so much of that dull black and gray. They make a blonde look too washed out."

"Yes, Mom. So you've told me."

"And that necklace is nice, too. Very stylish."

Julia smiled at her mother's backhanded compliment. All her life, Lucy had been coaxing her to wear "bold colors" and not look so "washed out." Also to "accessorize." Though her mother usually said it more like a battle cry—*Julia! Accessorize!*

Julia's tastes tended toward more subdued tones and few adornments. Especially for business meetings with bankers and lawyers. Her mother didn't seem to get it.

Today she'd been running an open house, and wore an outfit somewhere between "bold" and businesslike—a wrap-style burgundy sweater, a slim gray wool skirt and black boots. Not her usual mode of dress, but she was pleased her fashion-conscious mother approved of it. Lucy, as usual, was dressed stylishly, in a print dress of soft fabric with long sleeves, and slingback, high-heeled shoes. A bit fancy for their little one-on-one dinner, Julia thought. But she guessed her mother had probably been out today, at a luncheon or something. It didn't take much encouragement for Lucy to dress up.

Julia followed her mother into the kitchen and handed over the bakery box. "Here's some dessert, Mom. It should probably go in the fridge."

Lucy stared down at the box, as pleased and excited as a child. "Chocolate, I hope?"

"Do they even bake any other kind of cake, Mom?"

"They probably do. I never noticed." Lucy grinned and slipped the cake box into the refrigerator.

She took out a bottle of white wine and poured it out into two glasses that stood on the countertop, next to two platters of hors d'oeuvres.

"Try my dip," Lucy urged her. "It's goat cheese spread. A new recipe. Goat cheese is very…gourmet you know," Lucy added.

"So I have heard." Julia smiled and spread a taste on a cracker. She ate out a lot more than her mother and also watched a lot of cooking shows. She was a bit better versed on the current stylish foods. Her mother's idea of exotic cheese had always been a jalapeño cheddar. It was amusing to see her tastes branching out.

"Very good, Mom," she said, though she did wonder why her mother had gone to so much trouble for one of their weekly dinners. Julia picked up her wineglass. "This is a pleasant way to end the week. Cheers."

"Cheers, dear," Lucy touched her glass to Julia's. It made a faint, bell-like sound. They each took a sip.

Then Lucy peered up at Julia over the edge of her glass.

"I just have to heat the green beans and finish the table," she said. "Oh…and Lester is coming. He'll be here any minute." She added this last bit of information as if she'd just remembered.

Julia stared back, her expression resigned. She knew very well her mother had not just remembered. She was now sure this surprise guest star—her mother's latest beau, most likely—was the entire reason for the get-together.

"I don't remember you talking about a Lester lately, Mother."

"Lester Baxter? I talk about him all the time. You just haven't been paying attention, dear. I know when you call me from work you're listening with half an ear…or less."

Julia didn't answer. The accusation rang true. Though she needed a scorecard to keep track of Lucy's social life—even if she did pay attention.

"We've been seeing a lot of each other lately," Lucy added quickly. "He's very excited to meet you."

Oh, dear. This sounded serious. Julia took a large swallow of her chardonnay. She didn't want to overreact. That would only make her mother defensive.

"So…where did you guys meet?" She tried to sound casual and chatty, like a girlfriend, but knew it came out more like a friendly detective.

Her mother pulled open a cabinet door and began to take out dishes. "We met right here. In the kitchen. Romantic, right?"

Julia struggled to keep from rolling her eyes.

"Mom, you think everything is romantic. I suppose you'd think it was just divine if a guy came over to unstuff the garbage disposal."

Lucy stared at her a moment, then laughed. "Well, you must have been tuned in a few times when I spoke about him. You remembered that much."

Julia's mouth hung open. She'd meant it as a joke. A rather sarcastic one at that. Seemed the joke was on her.

"Lester repairs appliances?"

Lucy nodded. She went to the drawer next to the stove and counted out silverware. "Eleanor next door recommended him. The man I used to call, Stanley Alcott…? He retired. So when the disposal broke down, I called Lester. He came right over. Very prompt and polite. A real gentleman. Didn't leave any mess and he didn't overcharge. We got to talking, of course…." Of course there was talking, knowing her mother, who could learn a person's entire life story in the "ten items or less" line.

"He needed to order a special part and came back a few days later…."

Julia could just picture it. For Lester's second visit, her mother probably got a facial and a manicure and prepared a special lunch. Served on the good china.

She knew how Lucy operated once she had her eye on a man. Julia didn't need to hear any more.

"It's okay, Mom. I get the picture."

"We got along so well. So in tune. Right from the first."

Lucy shook her head, a soft smile lighting her face. Remembering those early moments of the courtship, Julia guessed, as Lester diagnosed and unclogged the ailing disposal, then lunched on Lucy's notorious "stuffed tomato."

Kismet.

"How long ago was that? When you met, I mean," Julia asked.

Lucy shrugged. She carefully rolled a linen napkin and slipped it into a shiny silver ring. "Let's see…about a month or so, I guess. It's hard to remember. It feels like I've known Les my whole life. I just feel so…comfortable with him."

Julia nodded, not daring to say a word.

This was how it always started.

Julia knew now she'd been right to suspect that something was going on. Lester Baxter was going on.

Julia picked up the tray with the dishes and silverware and carried it into the dining room, then helped her mother set up the table.

"How old is he?" she asked.

"A few years older than me. But not *too* old." Lucy glanced up briefly. Julia knew she was thinking about Earl T. Walker and his unfortunate demise.

"He's ready to retire. He's had enough of fixing appliances. But he wants to keep busy. Start a whole new business. He has some exciting plans. He's not one of these men who just want to loaf around under a palm tree and play golf for the rest of their life."

Julia knew her mother was talking about her ex-husband now, Julia's father. Perhaps Lucy had been widowed three times, if you count being a golf widow while married to Tom Martinelli.

The doorbell rang. Lucy set down the napkins. She flapped her hands in the air.

"That must be him, now. Come with me, Julia. Come say hello." She coaxed her daughter, tugging on Julia's sleeve as if she were nine instead of thirty-one.

Lucy smoothed her dress and quickly checked her lipstick in the foyer mirror. Julia thought her Mom looked great. As usual. For a woman in her late fifties, her mother still dressed with style and had a great figure—owing to her yoga and Jazzercise classes. She even still wore sexy high heels, the kind Julia mainly avoided due to her height and because they were so darned un-comfortable. Who was benefitting from all that agony anyway? Men, of course. Pure exploitation, Julia believed.

But Lucy didn't have a feminist bone in her body. Including her feet. She didn't understand what Julia meant, calling it ex-ploitation. She enjoyed being admired. "Isn't that what it was all about?" she'd once asked her daughter.

Julia had long ago given up trying to enlighten her. There was clearly no chance of changing Lucy's thinking at this point about the power struggle in male-female relationships. She obviously didn't think there was any.

Ready for the games to begin, Lucy pulled open the door with a welcoming smile that stretched from hoop earring to hoop earring.

The man on the other side of the door wore as smile just as wide.

Julia took in his looks with a glance. Medium height with a round face, bright blue eyes and a warm, friendly expression that distracted from his shiny bald head.

Nicely dressed, Julia thought. While she hadn't expected him to wear a uniform with his name on the pocket, the brown tweed sports coat, pale yellow wool vest and patterned tie looked rather country club-ish.

He was no movie star however. Not even an aging one. But not bad-looking, she amended. Most of all, Lester Baxter looked…friendly. Kind. Even patient. The type of man who would find her mother's eccentricities charming and endearing.

Julia wasn't sure how she could tell all that from just a glance. But she could.

He held out a huge bouquet of pink roses and offered them to Lucy. "Some flowers for the hostess."

He handed them down to her, looking eager to see if the gift was pleasing. Lucy accepted the bouquet with a radiant smile. "Lester…you shouldn't have. They're just beautiful."

"Just like you. You look like Miss America holding that bouquet, Lucy. I wish I had a camera," Lester teased.

"Oh, stop." Lucy shook her head, but Julia knew she was definitely enjoying the compliments and could have had him go on all night.

Julia sighed and rolled her eyes. This was worse than she imagined. Much worse.

"I brought you another surprise," he added. "I told you my son was coming down from Boston for a visit? Well, he got to town a little sooner than I expected. He pulled up to the house just as I was walking out the door, so I brought him along. I hope you don't mind?"

"Oh…of course not. Come in, come in…." Lucy stepped aside and Julia could see now that another man stood just behind Lester. He must have purposely been standing aside, waiting out of view.

Now he stepped into the light. He glanced at Lucy and smiled briefly. Then looked up, over Lucy's head, at Julia.

Their eyes met. Julia felt her mouth go dry, her heartbeat go from zero to a hundred and ten in two seconds flat.

Lester—the bald, paunchy, eager-to-please repair man—had fathered *that?*

Impossible.

Lester's son must have been adopted. He was without question the very definition of tall, dark and totally hot.

He stepped through the doorway, towering over all of them, Julia included. She rarely had to tip her head back to make eye contact with a man. But now she found herself staring up at him.

And they were all in such close quarters in the small entrance to Lucy's house. At least, it suddenly seemed much smaller and crowded, Julia thought. Draped in a dark leather jacket, his shoulders looked endlessly wide, his dark eyes looked endlessly deep.

"Sam, this is Lucy Martinelli. My Lucy," he added, with a meaningful glance at Julia's mother.

Sam Baxter held out his hand to Lucy and flashed a brief but brilliant smile. Julia blinked as the gesture transformed his features so completely from serious to something that was warm and full of light. Deep dimples creased the lean cheeks. His teeth were white and strong. Tiny lines fanned out at the sides of his eyes, a rich, dark, chocolaty shade of brown.

"Lucy…great to meet you. My father's told me a lot about you."

"And I've heard so much about you, Sam. I feel as if I already know you, dear," Lucy said.

Sam shook his head, looking almost boyishly embarrassed. He glanced at his father. "I hope he hasn't been boring you."

"I can't help bragging about my boy," Lester laughed and patted his son on the arm. "And this must be Julia. Lucy told me plenty about you, too, young lady…."

Lester turned to Julia. It seemed that everyone else had forgotten she was there.

Lester gave Julia's hand a hardy shake. "Good to meet you, dear."

"Nice to meet you, Lester." Julia smiled cordially.

It was hard not to like Lester. She made a sincere effort to match his enthusiasm—despite having only first heard of his existence five minutes ago.

She felt Sam Baxter staring at her. She looked up at him. No dazzling smile for her. To the contrary, his expression was serious again. His eyes, unreadable. He didn't offer his hand and introduce himself, and for some reason, she felt relieved instead of slighted.

"Sorry to barge in. My father insisted I stop by for a minute and say hello…."

Sam's apology was meant for her mother, Julia knew. Yet he addressed it to her.

She met his glance again. Just like the first time, she felt her mouth go dry, her polished conversation skills deserting her.

What in the world was going on here? When had she gotten so tongue-tied around a man? Silly… Had to be the wine. It had gone straight to her head. She'd never been able to drink on an empty stomach.

Before Julia had a chance to answer, her mother stepped forward and took Sam by the arm.

"Nonsense. Come inside and make yourself comfortable. You must stay for dinner. Lester, tell him he has to stay."

"Of course he'll stay," Lester insisted, following them.

The seniors were double-teaming him. He didn't stand a chance. He'd soon agree, Julia predicted, just to be polite.

The idea of spending the evening making small talk with Sam Baxter made Julia uneasy, but she brushed the feeling aside. She was just tired after a long workday, where she had to be polite and friendly to strangers all day at her job. Now she was forced to do it all night. Her annoyance had nothing to do with him.

"Well…maybe for a few minutes," Sam Baxter said.

"Wait 'til you try her cooking. You're in for a treat."

"Lester, please. Your son is in the business. He's not going to be impressed with my simple home cooking."

"Don't listen to her. You'll see. You'll be asking for her recipes," Lester promised.

Julia thought her mother was a good cook and Lester's lavish compliments were at least in the ballpark this time.

She wondered what Lester meant by Sam being in the business. Most chefs she'd ever met, even the younger ones, didn't have Sam's lean, fit body. Even the guys on TV. There was definitely something sexy about a man who cooked, though. An image of this man in chef's whites, an intimidating force in a hot, steamy commercial kitchen was very…distracting.

"Come. Sit down. Relax." Lucy herded everyone into the living room, though she didn't sit down herself, Julia noticed.

Sam sat on one end of the long pillow-back couch and Lester sat on the other. Julia took an armchair.

She crossed her long legs, then noticed Sam's eyes following her movement as she tugged her skirt down over her knee. Checking her out? She felt blood rush up her cheeks and hoped she wasn't blushing.

"I have some cheese spread and nibbles in the kitchen. I'll just run out and get them." Lucy glanced at Lester, who sat on the couch near Sam. Julia wasn't surprised when Lester quickly rose, as well.

"I'll help you, dear." Lester jumped up and followed Lucy like a loyal pet.

From the gleam in his eye, Julia guessed he was not only eager to help his hostess, but steal a little private time. Julia hoped they didn't take too long. For one thing, it could get embarrassing. For another, she already felt uncomfortable being left alone with the tall, dark and smoldering son.

Julia looked over at Sam. "They might take a while out there," he said quietly.

So he'd picked up on the same hints.

She glanced at him but didn't know what to say. A seasoned saleswoman, she was rarely at a loss on how to start a conversation. She'd even taught classes on the topic, for goodness' sake.

The polite thing to do would be to ask Sam what sort of work he did exactly, what had brought him down to Vermont from Boston. That sort of thing.

But some errant impulse caused her to start off on a completely different track.

"Did your father really tell you much about my mother? Or did you just say that to be polite?"

He looked surprised at her direct manner. But not at all offended. Maybe more like amused, she thought.

"The last few weeks, he hardly talked about anything else. It's Lucy, Lucy, Lucy. Why do you ask?"

Julia shrugged. She picked a thread off her skirt. "I didn't hear a word about your father until about fifteen minutes ago. Or maybe I did and I wasn't paying attention… Does your father date very much?"

His eyes narrowed. Now he did look a bit offended. Or at least, taken aback by her question. "Are you suspicious of his intentions? He's a very sincere person."

"I'm sure he's sincere. He's seem very nice. Really," she assured him. "My mother is very social. I just don't want him to get…disappointed."

She could tell he was definitely fighting a smile now. The corners of his mouth twitched and she nearly caught another glimpse of those devastating dimples. The entire gesture was utterly tantalizing.

"Don't worry about my dad. He's been out in the single scene a long time. He can take care of himself."

Lester might think he was the James Bond of the AARP set. His son might think so, as well. But they had never encountered the likes of Lucy.

She glanced toward the kitchen. No sign of the lovebirds. After they'd first disappeared, she'd heard them talking back there, but now there was only silence.

Bad sign.

She turned back to Sam, leaning forward a bit in her chair. "Do you think this is serious?" she whispered.

"Excuse me?" He leaned toward her, trying to hear what she was saying. They were suddenly face-to-face, closer than she expected. The scent of his spicy cologne filled her senses. His cheeks were shadowed by a day's growth of beard, lending a slightly scruffy and totally male edge to his handsome looks.

"I said…do you think it's serious? Between our parents, I mean."

"Looks pretty serious to me. They're crazy about each other. Haven't you noticed?" His deep, hushed tone was disturbingly intimate.

Julia leaned back and took a deep breath. She didn't know if she was more disturbed by the message or the messenger.

Julia sighed. She swept her long hair to one side, back over her shoulder. Again, she found him watching her, his eyes following the movement.

"My mother's been married…several times. Does your father know that?" she said finally, perhaps a bit sharper than she intended.

"He mentioned it. It doesn't seem to bother him."

"He'd be number five," Julia persisted, whispering as she glanced over her shoulder again.

He finally showed some reaction. His eyes widened. "That's quite a record. I'm not sure if he's done the math."

Now it was Julia's turn to sound defensive. "There have been good reasons why her relationships didn't work out. I mean, she was widowed twice. That certainly wasn't her fault."

"Of course not," he agreed, yet still looked wary.

Before Julia could say anything more in Lucy's defense, she heard the cooing twosome fluttering back into the room.

"So…you work in the restaurant business. Are you a cook or something?" she asked Sam in a loud, polite tone.

He looked straight into her eyes, signaling he was in sync with her cover-up. "Yes, I'm a chef. I've just left a position at a big restaurant so I could open my own place with a partner."

The independent type. Julia thought she should have guessed that. He looked like someone who didn't have the patience to take orders from a boss. From anyone, for that matter.

"That's sounds exciting," she said sincerely.

"It can be. Not always in a good way. My partner knows nothing about the business…except that he likes to eat out a lot. But I guess that's the reason a lot of rich people want to invest in a restaurant."

Sam smiled briefly, causing that curious buzz in her brain again. Julia valiantly shook it off.

She wondered how long he'd be in town visiting his father. But she didn't want to ask and sound too…interested.

What did it matter to her? She just had to get through the evening.

As if on cue, the older couple returned. Her mother set down the dish of cheese and crackers on the coffee table. Lester followed with the bowl of dip. Then they stepped back and stood side by side, as if performing a rehearsed dance step.

Lester glanced shyly at Lucy and took her hand. Lucy blushed and looked down at the floor.

Julia sat forward in her seat, her tingling intuition lighting up like a pinball machine.

"Kids…we have something to tell you," Lester began.

Julia cast a desperate look at her mother but couldn't catch her eye. Her gaze darted over to Sam, but he was staring at his father.

"We were going to wait. But since we have both of you here with us tonight, Lucy and I decided…"

Lester swallowed a big lump in his throat, his old eyes misting over. Julia nearly jumped out of her seat and shook him.

"Say it already!" she wanted to scream.

Then he did. Julia held her breath and felt an urge to cover her eyes with her hands, as if she were watching a horror movie.

"This lovely lady at my side has agreed to be my wife."

He turned to Lucy and planted a huge, wet, noisy kiss on her cheek. Lucy grinned, looking a bit tearful, too. She briefly hugged him. "Oh…Lester."

Then she met Julia's eye. Looking apologetic? More like a little kid who'd been caught doing something they shouldn't, but didn't want the teacher to be mad at them.

"Oh, Mom…you didn't…" Julia sighed.

Lucy may have answered. Julia wasn't sure. The image of her mother grew blurry…along with the rest of the room. She suddenly felt the room spinning and lifted her hand to her fore-head, afraid she might faint.

She struggled to remain upright in her chair but felt herself losing control. Pitching forward.

Everyone in the room shouted at once. Though she couldn't make out a word of it.

The last thing she remembered was her mother's carefully polished coffee table, coming closer. And closer...

Then a strange but wonderful sensation as—instead of a crash-landing into solid oak—she felt her limp body being caught and cushioned in the strong embrace of Sam Baxter.

## Chapter Two

"Julia? Sweetheart? Are you okay?"

Floating back up to consciousness, Julia heard her mother's voice. But saw only Sam's gorgeous face, his concerned expression, hovering above.

She seemed to be lying flat out on the living-room floor. On her mother's scratchy area rug. Sam was crouched on one side, her mother on the other.

"I'm all right," she insisted.

She tried to sound normal, but her voice came out shaky. She started to sit up, but Sam rested one big hand firmly on her shoulder. "Not so fast. What's the rush?"

She felt…mortified to have fainted dead away like that. She wished she could just crawl off into some convenient hole.

"I'd like to sit up now," she insisted.

Finally, Sam leaned back and let her go. Julia stared down at herself, then hurried to straighten out her clothing. During her flight, the wrap-style sweater had gotten unwrapped, exposing most of her lace-trimmed bra, and her skirt had hiked up to midthigh. She hurriedly covered herself, glancing sideways at Sam as she fussed. A twitch in his stoic expression revealed that he hadn't missed much.

*What else is going to happen tonight? Maybe my hair will catch on fire.*

"How about a glass of water?" Lester appeared behind Lucy and handed Julia some water. She took a long swallow, grateful for something to do while they all stared at her.

"I'm okay. Really. Probably just hungry. I skipped lunch," Julia explained, concocting a quick excuse.

Her mother still looked concerned. "Are you sure that's all it is, sweetheart? Does it hurt anywhere?"

Lucy lovingly felt Julia's forehead, the same way she had done all through her childhood. Julia felt a pang of love. How could she admit the real reason she'd fainted?

"I'm fine, Mom. Really."

"She works too hard," Lucy told the others. "Seven days a week. A regular workaholic—"

"Why don't we all just sit down and start dinner?" Julia interrupted, feeling even more mortified by her mother's diagnosis.

Julia started to stand up. Sam quickly stepped up beside her, slipping one arm around her waist and one under her arm to steady her balance. The contact was brief but electric, making her head spin all over again.

She caught her balance, then took a quick step away from him. But she couldn't help glancing back over her shoulder to make eye contact. It was hard to tell what he was thinking.

She wasn't sure she even wanted to know.

"Are you sure you feel up to it, honey?" Lucy stepped closer and put her hand on Julia's cheek. "Maybe we should call a doctor."

"No reason for that, Mother. Honest. Dinner is going to be ruined if we wait any longer. I'm sure you've been cooking all day."

Finally, Lucy gave in. "Okay, then. Into the dining room everyone. Julia's right. The roast will be all dried out if we wait any longer."

They were soon all seated in Lucy's dining room. Lucy sat across from Lester, and Julia sat across from Sam. A bottle of champagne appeared, and had probably been stashed somewhere in her mother's vast refrigerator. Her mother was always prepared for a romantic celebration, Julia thought.

"Let's start with a toast," Lester said. "I wasn't prepared with an engagement ring tonight. But this should make it official." He smiled as he filled everyone's glasses.

Julia covered hers with her hand. "No thanks, Lester. I don't think I can handle it right now."

She couldn't handle it physically. Or emotionally. And didn't want to be a hypocrite. The fainting spell had given her a perfect excuse to pass.

"I'll say a few words." Sam raised his glass, tilting it toward Lucy and Lester. "Though this announcement certainly comes as a surprise…and even a shock," he added, glancing briefly at Julia, "I think you're both old enough to know what's in your minds. And your hearts. It's a rare gift to find love. We need to cherish that gift. And run with it. Lucy, Dad, you're both very lucky to have found each other, and I wish you every happiness."

Julia was surprised. His toast was very touching, his words genuine and thoughtful. So, Sam Baxter was more than just a pretty face. She hadn't meant to do it, but found herself lifting her water glass and joining in.

"Thank you, son. That was very nice. I knew when I found Lucy, my life was complete," Lester said. "The only wish I have left now, is to see *you* with a true love of your own someday. Settled down. Giving me a few grandkids to spoil."

"Oh, me, too!" Lucy chimed in, as if Lester had mentioned that grandchildren were on sale this week at Kmart.

Sam shook his head, a faint blush coloring his lean cheeks.

Julia was glad that he was under the spotlight now and not herself. He did look totally adorable.

"Come on, Dad. This is your night. You know how I feel about that 'settling down' talk."

Lester laughed. "I know you tried it once and it didn't work out. That's no reason not to try again. Look at me and Lucy." He glanced at his bride-to-be. "We didn't give up just 'cause we didn't get it perfect the first time."

Julia's eyes widened. But she didn't say anything. She wondered if Lester really knew how many false starts his fiancée had under her belt. More than the shuttle launch at NASA.

So Sam had a failed relationship in his past, too. Julia found that tidbit of information interesting. It was hard to imagine a man who looked like that running around unclaimed. But it seemed his father had hinted as much.

Sam didn't reply. He took another sip of champagne. More like a gulp, Julia noticed.

"Pass the dishes, everyone," Lucy instructed. "Here, Sam. You start with the roast. And there's some gravy to your left. Lester…some string beans? I made them with the almonds, just the way you like."

"Looks delicious, dear," Lester said appreciatively. "Once we're married I'm afraid I'll gain fifty pounds."

"We have to keep active. That's the key. You can't just retire and loaf around. Watching TV all day."

"Not my plan at all. You know that," Lester said between mouthfuls.

Julia took some food on her plate and began to eat. Veal roast with tasty herbed stuffing, roasted potatoes and string beans. She was hungry, more than she realized.

"What are your plans, Lester?" Julia asked, curious to know. "My mother mentioned you want to start a new business?"

Lester nodded and dabbed his mouth with a napkin. "I'm going to just follow my bliss. Your mother and I, once we're married, are going to start a cheese-making business. Artisanal goat cheese. The secret recipe has been in my family for generations. I'm looking around for a good piece of property. Maybe you can help us out with that. I even have a pair of starter goats. Romeo and Juliet," he added with a grin.

He sent a sugary glance Lucy's way and they had soon joined hands on top of the table, gazing warmly into each other's eyes.

Julia lifted her gaze to the ceiling as she struggled to take it all in. So that explained her mother's new cheese dip recipe.

Was this a dream? Was it a joke?

Her mother, on a farm?

Making…goat cheese?

Julia sat back from her plate and took a deep breath, and then another. Her mother was hardly farm wife material. She didn't even like to garden. She'd have to fit her farm chores in between trips to the nail salon and pocketbook parties. As far as Julia knew, they didn't sell any outfits on QVC suitable for mucking out a barn.

Julia stared at Lester, wondering if he was kidding. But she could tell he was perfectly sincere.

"Well…these are big plans. You didn't tell me any of this, Mom," Julia said cautiously.

Lucy shrugged. "Lester's very organized. He's taken classes. And the recipe has been in his family for generations. There's a big demand for goat cheese these days. It's very gourmet."

"Yes…you mentioned that." Julia's voice was flat.

"Restaurants use a ton of the stuff. I think he can do very well."

Sam spoke up between bites. He met her gaze, his dark eyes issuing a faint challenge.

Julia countered with a withering look.

So, his true colors were finally showing. She could see where Mr. Handsome stood on this cheese question. Looked like three against one. She was alone in the battle to slow down this runaway train engagement and bring her mother to her senses about her fiancé's goat farm scheme.

Did Lucy really believe she could spend her golden years surrounded by a herd of nasty, smelly, braying…goats? Julia knew Lucy wouldn't last a week.

Obviously Lester had talked her into all of it. Her mother was so sweet and gullible. Especially when it came to men. A smooth-talking man who knew how to compliment her legs and her cooking could sell her the Brooklyn Bridge.

She'd bet anything the couple planned to finance the farm with Lucy's savings. Lester's contribution would be the secret family recipe.

Lester might appear to be just an affable old guy. But there was more going on in the bald dome than first impressions let on.

Miss America indeed. More like Miss Cash Cow.

Hopefully, this whole thing hadn't gone too far. It was hard to tell. All she knew was that Lester had a recipe and two goats.

Before she could ask any more questions, Sam changed the subject. "So, how did you two meet anyway? I don't think I ever got the whole story."

Lucy and Lester launched into a colorful narrative of their first meeting. Julia found her guess had been right. Lester did stay for lunch when he returned with the missing part for the garbage disposal. And Lucy had served stuffed tomato.

After some more family stories from her mother Julia had heard a million times before, dessert and coffee were finally served. Her mother brought in the towering chocolate cake, which was a big hit. Even Sam seemed impressed.

The look of sensual bliss on his face, eyes half-closed as he savored his first taste, gave Julia a fluttering feeling in the pit of her stomach. She quickly looked away, glad he hadn't caught her staring.

She accepted a larger than usual slice and ate every crumb. The decadent treat lifted her mood a bit. But not nearly enough.

Julia listened and waited but couldn't find an appropriate moment to ask more questions about the goat farm. She decided to corner her mother later, after father and son had left.

She had to find out how far things had gone.

And talk her mother out of it.

Saturday morning at 8:00 a.m., Julia marched down Main Street with two large coffees, a bran muffin for herself and a cranberry scone for Rachel. Rachel's shop, Pretty Baby, was at the very end of the street from the bakery, but Julia's long-legged stride reached her destination in no time.

The building had been in shambles when Rachel had bought it, but with Julia's help, she'd gotten a good deal. She'd renovated and restored it to being a showplace. Fearful of being overlooked at the end of the shopping route, Rachel had had the building painted in a fanciful, eye-catching combination of colors, a real painted lady, with a huge colorful garden that filled the front yard in the spring and summer. The garden was filled with the last of winter's snow now, a white backdrop for Rachel's hand-painted sign that read Pretty Baby Children's Boutique—Clothes, toys & furnishings. Made with a loving touch.

A small sign in the window said Sorry, Closed. But Julia knew the store was never closed to her. She didn't even need to knock before Rachel ran to let her in, her long, brown, curly hair bouncing around her shoulders as she opened the door.

"Are you okay?" Rachel's dark blue gaze took her in with a concerned look. "Your phone message sounded…"

"Insane? Stark-raving mad? Totally berserk?"

"How about all of the above. What's going on?"

"Lester Baxter. That's what's going on."

Rachel looked puzzled. "I'm sorry, I don't remember you ever mentioning him. Was he an awful date or an awful client?"

"My mother's new boyfriend. Her new *fiancé,* in fact. Lester proposed last night, in the kitchen, while they were supposed to be fetching the appetizers."

"So, Lucy's at it again." She shook her head. "You were right.

You said you had a funny feeling. What's he like? Did you like him at least? Is he nice?"

Julia shrugged and sighed. "He's nice enough, I suppose. Seems enchanted with Lucy. But they all do, at first. He seems to have patience, which is more than I can say for most." She flipped the lid from her coffee, then looked up at her friend. "I thought he was so sincere at first. I was actually afraid about Lucy disappointing him. Now, I'm not sure. I've started to suspect his paunchy, puppy-dog devotion might be an act. Try to tell my mother that. She'll never buy it."

"Why should she? Why would the man pretend to be in love with her and propose?"

"Lucy is quite comfortable. I ought to know, I manage her finances. Goodness knows, if she had to handle them herself, she'd probably have to move in with me. And rent a warehouse to store the shoe and handbag collection."

Rachel smiled. "She does like to shop."

"Lester's only known her a short time, but it's easy to get Lucy to tell all."

"So, he wants to marry her for her money? Is that what you think?"

"Lester's postretirement dream is to buy a farm, where they will raise goats and make gourmet cheese. From a secret family recipe."

Julia stared at Rachel over her coffee cup. "He and my mother have it all worked out. Except the part about wearing sling-back pumps in the manure pile."

"Your mother goes along with this?"

Julia nodded. "Uh-huh. He must have hypnotized her or something. I tried to talk to her privately about it, after they had left, but she wouldn't hear any objection. She's buying it, whole hog. Or rather, whole goat, I guess you'd have to say."

"Oh, dear…that is a nightmare. Poor Lucy. She's really gone off the deep end this time." Rachel paused and took a sip of her coffee. "How about Lester? Does he have any children?"

Julia wasn't sure if she should mention Sam Baxter, even to her very best friend in the world. Of course, if she started, she'd have to tell her everything.

"Lester's son, Sam, tagged along. He's visiting from Boston."

"Really? What's he like?"

Julia took a breath. "Well, let's see…. He's tall. Great body. Dark hair, sort of thick with a slight wave. A great face with these huge brown eyes. Oh…and dimples," she surmised in a flat objective tone. "Maybe the best-looking man I've been in room with?"

She swallowed a bit of bran muffin, but it stuck in her throat.

Rachel stared across at her, but Julia wouldn't meet her eyes. "Sounds too good to be true. Is he straight?"

Julia sighed. "Seemed straight as an arrow to me. I mean, I can't think of any other reason he'd be checking out my legs. And staring down my sweater when I fainted. You know, that wrap-sweater thing I bought last week when we were at the outlet mall?"

"Fainted? When did you faint?"

"I didn't black out totally. The big announcement sent me into shock. I sort of crumpled up and fell out of my chair. Then Superman swooped over and caught me in midair. Right before I cracked my head on the coffee table."

"Good reflexes."

"Yes, I thought so." Julia tried to make light of the episode.

"So, Lucy and Lester announced they were getting married. You fainted. Superman saved you from the coffee table…and then you heard about the goat farm?"

Julia tilted her head to one side. "That's a pretty accurate summary. Then father and son left and I tried to talk some sense into her. What a waste of time that was."

"Sounds like quite a dinner party."

"It was. Very memorable."

The two friends sat quietly. That was one of things Julia loved about Rachel's company. They didn't need to be chatting away incessantly every minute they were together.

"So, tell me more about this guy, Sam. Is he single?"

"He's not married. But that doesn't mean he's not attached. Men like that aren't running around loose. Believe me."

"That's what I thought about Jack when we first met," Rachel reminded her. "But here we are." She waved her left hand, showing off her wedding band.

Julia smiled at her. "You guys were meant to be. That's different. Sam must have been married, because Lester mentioned trying again. And giving him some grandchildren."

Rachel winced. "How embarrassing. How did he take it?"

Julia couldn't help but recall the faint blush on Sam Baxter's cheeks. "He just changed the subject."

"So what does Sam think?"

"He seems to support the entire situation. The marriage and the goat farm. So it's three against one. Tough odds for me. Especially since one of my main objections is that I suspect his father wants to marry Lucy just so she can buy him his farm."

"I guess stressing that point would not be the best way to win Lester's son over to your side," Rachel agreed. "Does he know how many times your mother has been married?"

"I tried to tell him, but I'm not sure it registered."

"Maybe if he knew more about Lucy, he'd be more wary of the situation. Concerned for his father."

"I thought of that," Julia said. She also thought how hard it would be to speak privately to him. Something about him seemed to totally unravel her.

"If he's visiting town for a few days, why don't you try to talk to him about it? Without Lester and Lucy around, of course. Maybe he'd flip to your side."

"I don't know. I might end up insulting him, being suspicious of his father's motives. Then they'd get married anyway and he'll always hate me."

"Well…that's one scenario," Rachel said, nearly laughing. "Does this guy make you nervous or something?"

Julia wasn't sure if it was nervous. Or something. Or all of the above.

"There's just something about him, Rachel. I don't know what it is. He's actually sort of quiet. Doesn't say too much. Laid back, watching everything…"

"Like legs crossing and sweaters slipping open?"

She knew Rachel was just teasing her and made a face. "You know what I mean. It's not anything he does in particular. But last night, I just couldn't think straight around him. Which of course, made everything worse. I'm still upset by all this crazy news. I'm not sure if I'm ready to deal with him yet."

"I'm not sure if I ever heard you say that about a guy, Julia."

Julia didn't answer. She was usually ready to take on anyone. But Sam Baxter wasn't just any guy.

"It's not just his looks," she said finally.

Okay, so he looked like a model in an ad for sexy jeans. Or shaving cream. Or maybe just plain old male virility, since that's what they were all really trying to sell anyway. All rugged angles and lean muscles and thick, shiny hair. That was part of it, for sure. But there was something more. Not so easy to put her finger on. And dismiss.

"There's something about him," she said with a shrug. "I'm not sure."

Some indefinable vibration she felt every time he so much as looked her way that got her rattled to the core. He didn't need to say a word.

Rachel stepped over to a display table nearby and started folding a pile of baby sweaters.

"Let's see," she said with mock seriousness. "Is it that thing they call…sexual chemistry? Could you, Julia Martinelli, battle-weary veteran of the dating wars, possibly be totally attracted to someone?"

Julia crumpled up the muffin wrapper, leaving half her daily requirement of fiber untouched.

"Of course he's attractive. I never said he wasn't. He's just…
not my type."

Rachel put down the sweater she was holding. "Explanation,
please? From the way you described him, if I wasn't already
married I'd ask for his number."

Julia shrugged. "Well, for one thing, he's a chef. They're all
drama queens. Believe me. Emotional, high-maintenance types.
I need someone more…low-key. Like me. And he obviously has
no common sense if he approves of his father marrying a woman
he hardly knows. I need to be with someone who's more logical
about things, like me." She shrugged. "Besides, this whole engagement situation between Lester and my mother makes
Lester's son totally off-limits. I mean, it's too complicated. It
would feel very awkward."

"I suppose," Rachel agreed reluctantly. "Awful timing if you
ask me. It's just that I haven't seen you light up this way just
talking about a new guy in ages. Too bad."

Julia didn't reply. Was she really "lighting up"? Gosh, that was
embarrassing. Even if it was only Rachel.

She didn't feel missing out on her chance to date Sam Baxter
was any great loss. She'd meant it when she'd told Rachel he
wasn't her type. Oh, she could see them getting involved all
right. There was definitely chemistry and she had a feeling,
they'd get very involved very quickly.

But it wouldn't last. How could it? They were definitely too different. She was businesslike and reserved. He was creative and
emotional. He lived in Boston and she was up here. The distance
alone was a big obstacle in and of itself. Even if she was interested.

Which she was not.

Yes, it was tempting.

But she couldn't afford to waste any more time on romances
that were exciting for a few weeks, but wouldn't lead anywhere.
At this stage of the game, she didn't have time to waste. Her
ovaries were on a tight schedule.

She stepped over to the clothing table and picked up a knitted cap with soft little white ears on top. She loved coming into this store—and hated it sometimes, too.

The clothes were so sweet and dear, she could almost cry, picturing a chubby-cheeked little baby in the cap, for instance. Tying the strings under its little chin, not too tight, and not too loose. A baby that would be her own.

But didn't yet exist.

Would he or she ever exist?

She felt Rachel touch her arm lightly and she put the hat down.

"Julia, I feel for you. You're in a tough spot. I know your mother. She's lovable and dear. But difficult sometimes, too. I understand how you feel responsible for her." Rachel paused. "But…she might need to do as she wants and make her own mistakes, you know?"

Julia felt as if they were talking about a teenage daughter instead of her mother. But she could see Rachel's point.

"Yes, I know. But it's hard to watch her keep making the same mistakes over and over again. I mean…one description of insanity is repeating the same action and expecting a different result. You know, like banging your head against a wall?"

Rachel's expression was thoughtful. "Well, I guess you could say that's the same description of trying to find someone to love. Sometimes it does feel like you're banging your head against a wall. At least, that's the way I remember it."

Julia didn't know what to say. There was no way to argue with the dyed-in-the-wool romantic. Backed in a corner, they always answered on totally unrealistic terms. Julia didn't think like that.

"I'm sorry, Jules," Rachel added. "Like I said before, I know you're in a tough spot. And I'm definitely on your side. So it's *two* against three, okay?"

Julia nodded and smiled. "Thanks. I know."

Julia heard a sharp knock. They looked up to see two women peering through the window. Julia glanced at her watch. "Nine on the dot. They're clamoring to get in here and buy stuff. I wouldn't keep them waiting."

"Don't worry. I didn't plan to."

Rachel trotted over to the door and pulled it open, wearing a welcoming smile. "Good morning, ladies. I'll be right with you."

Julia had followed her. "I'd better get to work myself. Thanks for letting me vent."

"Don't be silly, what are friends for?" Rachel leaned over and gave her a hug. "Call me later if there are any new developments."

"Fasten your seat belt," she added. "It's going to be a bumpy ride."

Rachel's answering smile made Julia smile, too, though inside she felt her prediction was bound to come true. It was no laughing matter, these hasty marriage plans and the goat farm idea, to boot.

But if she didn't try to laugh at it, at least a little, Julia was afraid she might cry.

Julia marched down Main Street toward her office. Had the entire world gone off the deep end, believing anything was fine and dandy as long as two people claimed to be in love?

It almost made a person feel nostalgic for a bygone day, when marriage was a much more formal arrangement. Like a business negotiation. Between the parents, primarily. A bride and groom sometimes didn't meet until the wedding day and notions like romance and love didn't figure in at all.

At least back then, if a man was marrying a woman for her fortune—or vice versa—people were honest about it.

Thinking of the days of arranged matches reminded Julia that she'd forgotten to pick up Rachel's copy of *Pride and Prejudice,* which they were reading for their book group this month. She had no plans for tonight and was looking forward to a relaxing evening by the fire, reading a cleverly written classic. She'd have to call Rachel and figure out how to pick it up. She didn't have many days left to finish it.

Julia found herself passing the Blue Lake General Store. She needed another cup of coffee before she started work. And even something else to eat. Her daily bran muffin just hadn't done it for her. She craved something sweet and buttery and loaded with fat grams and carbs. The bad kind.

This was a state of emergency. She was allowed to fall off the fiber wagon once in a while.

Ella Krueger stood behind the counter and greeted her with a wide smile. The coffee line was usually long at this time in the morning on a weekday, but there were only a few people— workmen mostly on their way out to a building or painting job— waiting for breakfast sandwiches, which Ella's husband was cooking up on a grill.

"Coffee, Julia?"

"Yes, please. Large black."

"Anything else today, hon?"

Julia tried to resist the tempting offerings in the breakfast pastry case.

Then she saw it. Crumb cake. Ella's own, homemade and fresh from the oven. "I guess I'll have a piece of crumb cake. Not too big though," she added quickly.

Ella laughed. "We only give out big pieces here. Did you know my crumb cake is a prize winner at the county fair? See, it's hanging up there," she said, pointing to a plaque. "Best crumbs, five years running. Most people can't get them that big. They fall apart. Mine stay big. And they stay on the cake. It's a secret recipe."

Julia wasn't surprised. There seemed to be a lot of secret recipes in this town.

Ella rang up the sale and Julia handed over some money.

"Well, I won't try to guess. But it is delicious."

"What's delicious?"

Julia turned her head slightly. Sam Baxter was standing close by. She wondered how long he'd been there, watching her. Rude of him not to make himself known and just stand there…spying. She did feel caught in the act, the damning evidence in her hand.

"The crumb cake. It's very good. Ella makes it herself."

"Prize-winning crumbs?" he asked.

He was a gourmet chef, Julia realized. He probably thought Ella's pride was cute but misplaced. Julia felt annoyed at him on Ella's behalf. But she knew that wasn't entirely it.

"How long have you been standing there?"

"Not too long." The corner of his mouth twitched and he nearly smiled. "I'm sorry…I didn't mean to sneak up on you. I just came out for a walk and wanted some coffee."

"She makes good coffee, too. Enjoy."

Julia cast him her best real-estate-lady smile and nodded, then tucked the newspaper under her arm and turned to go.

He watched her for a moment, then quickly tried to catch up. She was just about out the door when he finally did.

"I'm glad I ran in to you…I thought we should talk, if you have a minute."

He stood very close, staring down at her, his hands dug into the pockets of his leather jacket. The wind lifted a few strands of his dark hair and blew it across his eyes. She had the wild temptation to reach up and push it back for him.

"Sorry…I've got to get over to my office and open up. Saturday is very busy."

Which was partly true. But since it was the doldrums of the winter, there wasn't much going on and several employees had keys.

Julia picked up her pace, hoping to lose him. Most men, even tall ones, had trouble keeping up when she did her speed walk.

He didn't seem to notice and kept up easily. It appeared to be his preferred pace.

He wore the same leather jacket he'd worn last night, she noticed, with jeans. A gray sweater showed underneath and a brown wool scarf was slung around his neck.

Julia had hoped her reaction to his looks had been a fluke. But all in all, he looked just as sexy and appealing as he had last night. Maybe even better, if possible.

Finally, they reached the realty office. Julia felt a bit winded and felt a slight sheen of sweat on her forehead, but tried not to show it.

He stared up at the sign painted on the storefront window. "Home Sweet Home Realty. Cute." He smiled at her. But she didn't smile back. "I didn't take you for the type to go for cute."

"It's memorable and sets a comfortable tone." Julia sometimes thought the name of her business was *too* cute. But she didn't need him pointing that out to her.

She approached the door, key ring in hand. But her assistant, Marion McKenzie, had already arrived and opened up, making her feel a bit foolish for acting so urgent.

"Looks like someone beat you to it. Too bad, you were really moving. Were you on the track team in college?" Sam sounded mildly amused.

"Tennis," she said shortly. "I have a wicked serve."

"I wouldn't doubt it."

She dumped the keys back in her purse. She glanced up at him, prepared to make another excuse about getting to work. But her curiosity got the better of her.

"So, you want to talk about our parents. Have you changed your opinion about their engagement? You seemed pretty supportive last night."

"And you're definitely not. At least that's what your mother says. She called Lester this morning at the crack of dawn." He made a face. "She says you're very upset and demanded that she call it off."

Julia felt awkward hearing her words tossed back at her. Especially by him. He made her sound like some sort of shrew.

"I am upset. But I never demanded anything. I know my mother. She's like…like a cat. You just don't get very far delivering ultimatums. I never said call it off. I did say slow it down."

"So you do have reservations," he said, choosing his words carefully. "Some strong reservations."

"Of course I do. For one thing, they hardly know each other.

And this goat farm idea…it's totally absurd. My mother wouldn't last one week on a farm that grows costume jewelry, no less one filled with animals. To think for one minute that she could…that just goes to show how little your father really knows her."

His eyes narrowed. She hadn't meant to sound so harsh, but somehow she couldn't control it. Somebody had to face facts around here. It seemed as if she was the only one who would.

"I don't know your mother. I do know my father. He's a good man. Solid. Dependable. If he says he's going to do a thing, he'll do it. He's talked about this venture for years. He's taken classes. He's done research. He's visited farms just like it. It's not just some pie-in-the-sky fantasy."

"All right. I'll buy all that. But tell me this. If he's been dreaming about this cheese business for so long, why hasn't he gone ahead and started it? Is it because he never had the capital?" she said quickly, before he could speak. "Of course, if he marries my mother, that sticky little problem is solved, isn't it?"

As soon as she'd said the words aloud, Julia immediately regretted her frankness. Sam's face got pale as paper, then colored red. His dark eyes flashed, and he seemed to be closer, looming over her. She tried to look away but couldn't.

They stood staring at each other in a silent stalemate for a second and she realized that if he'd been an unleashed dog, she would have run for cover.

"How dare you. My father is an honest, honorable guy. He doesn't need to marry your mother for money. In fact, she seems a bit high-maintenance to me. I think he's going to have his hands full. But he says he's in love. I'm not debating him about it."

Now he was taking shots at her mother. She could have predicted that. She wasn't going to be intimidated by him. She wasn't going to back down. She suddenly wished she had on higher heels so she could stare him right in the eye.

"He has the funds to start the business on his own?" Julia persisted. "Is that what you're saying? Why hasn't he done it yet then? Why hasn't he…followed his bliss? Why did he need to wait for my mother to arrive on the scene?"

He didn't answer right away. Either she'd made him even madder or she'd backed him into a corner. Or both.

"He's been waiting to retire," he said finally. "That's one reason. And you're right. He doesn't have all the funds in hand. But he'd be able to borrow it. That wouldn't be a problem. People get loans to start up businesses all the time. I thought you were a big hotshot real-estate broker. You should know that."

Julia tried not to smirk but it was hard. She knew all about financing and loan qualifications. Loan officers were not scrambling to get their hands on retirees with no income and little assets who were starting up farms.

Maybe at Bank of Dumbbell Lenders. But not at most banks.

She decided not to infuriate him any further with this point. What was the sense? This conversation had gone far enough. She crossed her arms over her chest and took a breath.

"Are we finished? I need to get to work. I can see we disagree on this matter and are not about to find any common ground very soon. If ever."

She could tell from his expression he didn't like being brushed off. She guessed it probably didn't happen very often.

"I can see that you're a very rigid, uptight and close-minded woman. The packaging is definitely…misleading. I'll grant you that."

Julia drew in a sharp breath. Rigid and close minded? Is that what he thought of her? Just because she dared to call it for what it was? He had some nerve.

"Fine. That's just fine," she snapped back angrily. "I can see that you're as illogical, impractical and naive as…as…my mother. And *that's* saying something!"

His mouth opened, then closed again. He'd probably been about to carry the argument further, then thought better of it.

"At least I know where you stand."

"Same here," she responded. "See you around."

She pushed open the door to her office and stepped inside, not daring to look back. She felt shaken and tired from the confrontation. Luckily, none of the sales staff had arrived yet. She walked down the aisle between the row of desks that filled the main room.

Marion sat at the back, near the door to Julia's office. She looked up from her computer and smiled. "Morning, Julia. Who was that guy you were chatting up? New client?"

"He's just…some guy. He's just…an idiot. That's who he is."

She knew Marion wouldn't understand but it felt good just to vent.

Marion gave her a look, then turned back to her computer screen. "Um…okay then. You had some messages."

Marion handed her a wad of pink messages slips. Julia took them without thinking.

"Thanks," she said quietly. She unlocked the door to her office, then suddenly noticed the bag of crumb cake in her hand.

She'd totally lost her appetite. Her stomach was churning in a ball of knots.

"Marion…would you like some crumb cake? Ella Krueger's. The prize-winning crumbs."

Marion looked cheered by the offer. "Gee…thanks. I would. I didn't get breakfast yet."

"Here you go. Enjoy." Julia handed it down. "And thanks for coming so early and opening up."

Marion looked surprised. "Oh, sure. No problem."

Julia nodded and smiled. She paused at the half-open door.

"Marion, you've known me a long time now. Would you say that I'm…uptight…or small minded?"

Marion considered the question a moment. Longer than Julia thought necessary. Finally she shook her head.

"Uh, no. I don't think so. Not really."

Not really? Wasn't that like saying "almost"?

Julia sighed. She had to take what she could get.

"How about rigid? Do you think I'm rigid?"

Marion stared at her. "Well, you're a very good business-woman, Julia. You're very assertive and tough. You really stick to your guns." She smiled, looking puzzled by the question. "I don't know if I'd call that rigid. To me it's more like persistent."

Assertive. Tough. Persistent.

Weren't those terms all just nice ways of saying rigid? Julia decided to check the thesaurus.

"Well…thanks. Enjoy the crumb cake."

Julia turned, stalked into her office and closed the door. She should have quit while she was ahead.

## *Chapter Three*

Julia hid out in her office for the rest of the day. She had received a few phone messages, mostly from her mother, but put off returning the calls.

She wasn't ready yet to talk to Lucy. She didn't want to get into another argument today. But on the other hand, she didn't want to say anything that Lucy might misinterpret as a vote of support for her ill-advised plans.

Julia remained rattled and weary from her battle with Sam Baxter. Luckily, it was slow today and her only appointments with clients had been canceled. She didn't feel much in the mood to put on a happy face.

She had a pile of paperwork on her desk and buried her head in it, like a highly business-minded ostrich. Work was her foolproof remedy for all kinds of emotional upsets and this situation was no different.

Today, for some reason, it wasn't working.

Images of Sam Baxter's scowling—yet still somehow incredibly handsome—face kept floating into her thoughts. Like pop-up ads on the Internet. She wished she could somehow program her brain to block them out.

So, he thought she was rigid, and what?

Close minded.

Oh, and uptight.

That one made her wince. It was a word men used when they thought women weren't very sexy. He might as well have called her a spinster. Or a prude. Julia got angry all over again, every time she recalled his final, parting blow.

"The packaging was misleading," he'd said. Did that mean he thought she was physically attractive at least?

Or maybe he didn't mean that at all, just that she didn't look like someone who was rigid and close minded.

Oh, well. What did it matter. He despised her now.

Just as well, she coached herself gruffly. The reservations she'd explained to Rachel were definitely valid. Getting involved with him was just too awkward and complicated under the circumstances. Not that there was a snowball's chance in a sauna now that they ever would.

She considered calling Rachel to report on the disastrous meeting. But Rachel was always crazy busy in her store on Saturday. Julia didn't want to bother her. Besides, it was practically too embarrassing to relate.

Marion left soon after lunch. Her daughter had a basketball game. Julia didn't mind, but she didn't pick up her own phone when it rang, just left it on voice mail.

It was nearly five when her mother called again.

"Julia? It's me. I guess you're very busy today at work. Give me a call when you get a minute, will you? I've been thinking it over and I guess it wasn't very considerate of Lester and me to spring our announcement on you like that…."

Julia felt herself softening at the sound of her mother's

penitent tone. She had called two times before. And she did sound as if she was starting to understand Julia's side of it.

But before Julia could pick up the phone, Lucy added, "I know how you hate surprises. You always did, even as a little girl."

Hate surprises?

She didn't hate surprises! She wasn't that…uptight.

She didn't like manipulative little schemes designed to catch her off guard and blindside her.

That's what she didn't like.

The kind of scheme her mother had sprung on her last night, for instance.

"Anyway, give me a call when you have a chance. I'd like to hear from you, dear. You know, no matter what. I'm still your mother."

And what was that supposed to mean? Whenever they got into some little tiff, her mother would always say that. As if it solved everything.

*As if I could ever forget.*

She heard her mother hang up and the message ended. Julia's chin flopped in her hand. She sighed and twirled a long strand of hair around her finger.

She tried to focus again on the mortgage chart she'd been working with, but the numbers grew blurry and mixed-up.

It was time to go home. Back to her lovely but empty house. A renovated farmhouse that had been in shambles when she'd found it. She'd picked it up cheap and had taken her time restoring it. Room by room. She knew every workman and builder in town, so had found the best help and advice.

It had all turned out perfectly, though her secret plan had been to find someone to share it with her by now. That was a home improvement that just couldn't be ordered at the lumberyard or home improvement warehouse store.

Best of all, she loved her perfectly renovated kitchen, where she liked to try out complicated recipes she saw on TV cooking shows or have friends over for dinner.

But she often felt it was too much bother just for herself.

As she drove through town, she had her pick of take-out stops, but decided that she wasn't very hungry. She'd just make herself something easy, one of those frozen meals-for-one she had stacked in the freezer, then cuddle up in her sweats and read her book group novel. She'd called Rachel about it and her friend had promised to drop the book off tonight on her way home from town.

She'd read it back in school, but realized now she hadn't appreciated it. A woman needed experience with men to savor this story. She saw the story now in a new light and loved the way Elizabeth Bennett gave Mr. Darcy his comeuppance.

Though in real life, speaking frankly and boldly to a man didn't end up with him groveling at your feet. It ended up with him calling you…rigid, uptight and close minded.

A short time after she got home, Julia had showered, pulled on a comfortable black velour sweatsuit and put her wet hair back in a high ponytail. She spread some julep facial on her nose and cheeks and let it set while she popped a "Fit & Tasty" meal-for-one in the oven and set the timer.

It was a bit depressing to be alone on a Saturday night, waiting for a slice of low-fat lasagna to defrost. It made her feel a bit like a loser. She made a fire in the hearth in the family room that adjoined the large luxury kitchen. Then she lit a few candles, making the house look warm and inviting. Just the way she'd fix it for company. Didn't she deserve to have it looking just as comfortable and relaxing?

That was the problem with living alone, she thought. One of the problems. You had to learn how to take care of yourself. To treat your poor single self as nicely as you would…a man who came to visit, who you didn't know from beans.

Why should you pamper and impress some stranger and not

be just as nice to yourself? Julia asked herself as she walked around and lit the scented candles.

She tried to focus on the positives in her life; she made a mental list. She was smart, attractive, successful, fun to be with and a generous friend. She didn't need a man to make her feel worthwhile or validated. How many times had she forced herself to go out on dates that were pointless and boring? It was much better to be alone than go through that kind of torture.

*When the right man comes along, I'll know,* she promised herself. *Until then, I can just hang out in my lovely house and enjoy my own company...and my own scented candles.*

She heard the doorbell ring. It had to be Rachel, dropping off the novel. She must have forgotten to do it on her way home and was backtracking. Thoughtful of her. Maybe she'd be able to stay for a few minutes and chat.

Julia ran to answer the door as the bell sounded again.

"Coming..." She knew she looked a complete mess, no make-up and her wet hair coming loose from the clip. But it was just Rachel. She wouldn't care.

Julia pulled open the door with a big friendly smile.

Rachel was not there. It was Sam Baxter, standing with hands at his sides, his head bowed a bit, the rugged lines of his face shadowed by the porch light.

She was so shocked to see him she couldn't even say hello.

"Sorry to come by like this, unannounced. I would have called you first. But your number is unlisted."

"Yes, for a reason."

Julia knew she didn't need to be so snide with him. But she couldn't help herself. He ignored her tart reply.

"Are you busy? Having a costume party or something?"

She realized then why he was grinning and thought his joke so funny. The green stuff on her face.

"Oh..." She felt herself blushing with embarrassment under

the facial mask, which had now dried so hard and stiff she could barely crack a smile.

"This is the special treatment I use to keep my smile nice and rigid. And uptight."

He winced. "I deserved that."

"Yes, you did. Okay, we're even now. Feel better? You can go."

He tilted his head to once side, making no move to go, Julia noticed. He actually came a bit closer, edging himself into the doorway.

"Actually I came to apologize. The way I acted toward you this morning…well, I was totally out of line. I know that you care about your mother and you're only trying to speak up for her best interests."

Julia was surprised. She felt a genuine smile starting to form, but it was blocked by the facial mask.

"Well…thanks. I said a few things, too, that were…out of line. So I apologize, too."

Not that she didn't still suspect his father of finding a convenient way to finance his goat farm. But no reason to start hashing that out again.

She didn't know what else to say. The thought of inviting him in darted through her mind. But she slapped it down like a pesky mosquito.

"Well…thanks for dropping by. I've got to go. I have something cooking."

"Yes…I think I smell it burning…."

Julia turned her head. She smelled it, too. "Oh, blast." She turned to see a black plume of smoke floating out to the living room.

Suddenly the ear-piercing shriek of the smoke alarms filled all the rooms. Julia ran to the kitchen, leaving Sam standing at the open door.

She found smoke leaking out from around the oven door. She checked the oven temperature and saw that she'd set it much too high. She opened the door and a huge gust of black smoke filled the room.

She felt her eyes tear and began to cough. Her meal-for-one was charred black. Meanwhile the alarms continued to shriek insanely, so that it was impossible to think.

"Here, let me. I'm used to this." He had grabbed a dish towel, wrapped it around his hand and took the entire mess out of the kitchen and through the glass slider to the deck off the family room.

Julia fanned the air with her hand, but it was hard to see and she was coughing so much, she could hardly breathe. She made her way over to the smoke alarm, got up on a chair and tried to shut it off. She reached up, but missed the button. Then she jumped again, this time higher.

Sam was standing below. "Watch out. You're going to fall."

He reached up and steadied her, just as she finally pushed the reset button and shut the darned thing off.

Julia sighed with relief. Then she felt another coughing spell overcome her. This time she did feel herself losing her balance and cried out loud. "Whoa…"

Sam quickly grabbed her around her hips. She rested her hands on his shoulders and found herself sliding down his body.

What a ride! Some irreverent, sex-starved part of her brain reveled in the body-to-body contact.

His body was long, lean and hard and her soft curves seemed to fit the hard lines of his torso—and even lower—perfectly.

When she finally landed, they were both stunned speechless and just stood holding each other for a long moment.

Sam blinked. Julia coughed, then quickly stepped away.

"Thanks," she mumbled.

"Sure. No problem," he muttered. At least he seemed as affected as she did, she noticed.

"You seem to keep catching me from crash landings," she observed, trying to make a joke.

"Just lucky, I guess." He grinned at her, looking composed again.

She wasn't sure if he meant that she was lucky to have him catch her, or he was lucky to be doing the catching. He was still looking at her, a curious expression on his face.

She felt self-conscious and turned to the sink to wash the grime off her hands. Then she took a wet paper towel and quickly swabbed what remained of the green facial from her cheeks and nose. It had gotten so dry, most of it had flaked off already. At least she hoped it had.

"Was that your dinner?"

She nodded, thinking the burned lasagna must have looked quite pathetic to him. When he wanted something fast, he probably whipped up a salad with roast duck comfit, or a wrap with grilled vegetables and exotic mushrooms or something.

"I wasn't very hungry. I'll just grab a yogurt."

"I can cook something for you. For us. I didn't have dinner, either."

Julia was surprised by the offer. She didn't know what to say. "Really. You don't have to go to all that trouble…." she began.

"It's no trouble. Besides, I feel responsible. If I hadn't distracted you, your dinner wouldn't have burned," he pointed out.

The truth was, she burned food all the time. But she didn't admit that to him. He was a major distraction, that part was true.

"Consider it a peace offering? We got off on the wrong foot today. This would be a good chance to start over."

Julia met his dark eyes. The coaxing expression on his handsome face was very persuasive. It was hard to put him off. Hard to insist that she'd really had a long day and really wasn't hungry.

Then her mother's words rang in her ears. *You never liked surprises. Even as a little girl.*

This is a surprise, Julia. One of those things that happen that you don't expect.

Are you going to get all uptight and close minded about it, huh?

Julia shook her head in a distracted way. "Well…all right. If you really want to. I don't have much in the house," she warned him. "It might be a challenge."

"I always wanted to be in one of those cooking contests where they give you a platter of odd ingredients."

"Here's your chance to practice. I promise my refrigerator is stocked with odd ingredients."

He laughed. Those dimples and straight white teeth again. Resisting him was going to be the big challenge here.

He opened a few cabinets and scanned the contents. "Chicken broth. That might come in handy…. Basmati rice…nice… Oh, some saffron." He pulled out the small vial of orange spice threads from her spice closet, looking impressed.

"I bought it but I never used the stuff," she confessed.

"Well, it might be just what we need tonight," he promised. He put some food items out on the counter and continued rummaging. Julia stood back, trying to compose herself.

What did you just do?

Did you actually give this man permission to stay, to ransack your kitchen, then hang out here, cooking for you?

Do you really think that's a good idea?

It was a terrible idea. And seemed even more terrible as he slipped off his leather jacket, pushed up the sleeves of a black V-necked pullover and she found herself studying the muscles in his arms and shoulders, outlined under his thin wool shirt.

But he'd been so nice about stopping by to apologize and then putting out the burning lasagna. It was hard to say no.

*I can control myself. Don't worry,* she argued back.

Right. Like the way you body-surfed down his private parts?

He suddenly turned and met her glance. Julia was caught by surprise, staring at him.

"Do you have a large, heavy skillet?"

Her kitchen was well-equipped with state-of-the-art appliances and cookware. Even though she wasn't much of a cook, she enjoyed it and always wanted to do more. When she had the time and a good reason. Like…when she had a family.

"The skillet is hanging on that rack, right above your head," she said, pointing it out.

"Great. Mind if I open a bottle of wine?" He looked over the wine rack and pulled out a bottle. "I might need it for the recipe."

Good line. She'd never heard it before. Very original.

"Sure. I'll get some glasses."

She set out two glasses and he opened a bottle of white wine. The cork emerged with a popping sound. Then he poured some into each of their glasses. "Here's to…an interesting challenge."

She knew he meant cooking a dinner out of the spare pickings in her kitchen, but when he caught her eye over the rim of his glass, she couldn't help thinking he also meant her. Was she presenting a challenge to him? She hoped so. He'd come here to apologize for calling her names in the middle of Main Street. But also, obviously, believing he could charm her. Win her over. Smooth things out for his father.

She definitely liked him. And found him charming. Not to mention over-the-top attractive. But he wasn't going to change her mind about the ill-advised marriage plans. Or erase her suspicions.

She took a quick sip, careful not to drink too much. She had skipped lunch today and didn't want to faint into his arms again. Or worse.

"Can I help you with anything?" she offered.

He poured a bit of oil in the sauté pan, then began slicing a clove of garlic. "Let's see…I found a few mushrooms in the vegetable drawer."

"Really? Were they growing in there, or did they look store bought?"

He laughed. "Store bought. Though the wild ones can be very tasty." He glanced over his shoulder at her briefly. "Can you clean and slice them for me?"

"No problem." Julia located the forgotten box of mushrooms

on the counter, where all the possible ingredients he'd found were piled.

She reached over to grab the box and felt herself brush against his body, hip to hip. He peeked over his shoulder at her a moment and she quickly stepped over to the sink.

Once she got the sink spray going on the mushrooms, she felt like spraying herself down, too.

The oil in the sauté pan sizzled as the appetizing scent of garlic filled the air. Julia concentrated on her task, washing and carefully patting dry the mushrooms. Then she carried the bowl and a chopping block over to the island counter and sat a stool across from the stove, as far as possible from her new private chef.

"Nice kitchen. Do you cook much?" he asked.

"Not as much as I'd like," she admitted. "When you're one person, it doesn't seem to make much sense. I mean…unless you're a professional."

"I eat at the restaurant mostly. I keep pretty long hours. When I come home I'm beat. A bowl of cold cereal is about all I can handle."

For some reason, the image of this big brawny guy eating a bowl of cereal made her smile.

"Nothing too sugary I hope?"

"Anything with a toy surprise inside," he teased her back.

He sautéed a few boneless chicken breasts Julia had stocked in the freezer and set them aside on a platter. The he added some chopped onion and garlic. "I'm ready for the mushrooms now."

Julia brought them over and set them on the counter. She could have retreated back to her stool, with the granite-top island between them. But instead, she stayed nearby, sipping her wine as she watched him work.

He seemed to be totally focused now, cooking the mushrooms in the onion mixture, then tossing in a pile of rice and sautéing that, as well, seasoning and shaking the skillet with a professional touch she'd seen only on TV cooking shows. Then he added half a bag of frozen shrimp he'd found in the freezer, quickly poured in the broth and some wine, stirred and then covered the pan.

There was a real economy in his movements, a certain rhythm that was mesmerizing. She would not get bored of this show very quickly, she realized.

"Now for the saffron, the crowning touch...." He took a few small threads and blended them into the mixture, then covered the pan again.

The kitchen smelled glorious and Julia's stomach was growling with hunger as she fixed a bowl of green salad. She always had bags of that on hand, the kind that was already washed and cut up.

She set two places for them to eat on the granite-top island. When she was just about done, she noticed that Sam had added some other items to the pot and tossed in the cooked chicken, sliced in bite-size pieces. He stirred it all up, added more seasoning, then spooned it all out on a large platter, scattering some chopped parsley on top.

"Wow, that looks great. I think I missed a few steps though."

He smiled at her. "I think I skipped a few steps. It's sort of an impromptu paella. But it should taste okay."

If it tasted anywhere near as good as it smelled, Julia knew this was going to be delicious.

Sam brought the platter to the table and they sat down opposite each other. Julia put some food on her plate and so did he.

He watched her, obviously waiting for her to try it. She felt pressured by his scrutiny. What if it was awful and she wanted to spit it out in a napkin? She forced a smile and took a small bite, then felt relief that she didn't have to fake her reaction one bit.

"Hmmm. This is fantastic...."

He looked at her, one eyebrow raised, as if doubting her praise.

"Really. It's delicious. I never had mushrooms in paella before though."

"Oh, right. That was a sudden inspiration. You worked so

hard slicing them, I didn't want to leave them out and make you feel bad," he admitted.

She smiled at his admission. "Saffron has always intimidated me. I guess it's not so hard to use after all."

"It's a no-brainer."

"Maybe for you, pal," she said, laughing at him.

He smiled back warmly, looking pleased at her compliments.

"Cooking is not as complicated as some people think. Or, for that matter, as some cooks make it look. It's a matter of mastering some basics, and then variations on a theme. Going with what you have on hand or find at the market that day. Being creative. Flexible."

Julia nodded. All the qualities he seemed to think she lacked.

"I think it's practice, too. Maybe I should cook more and not just wait until…" Until I have a man and a family, she nearly said. "Until I have more spare time. I mean, you just have to make the time for things you enjoy, right?"

He glanced up at her and met her eye. "Yes, exactly."

"What kind of food will you serve at your new restaurant?" she asked, trying to change the subject.

"My partner is pushing for a Cajun-themed menu, sort of a party-hardy New Orleans atmosphere. I'm pushing for something quieter. I'd prefer a classic American menu, changing with the seasons so we can use what's freshest and most available at the market."

He looked distressed. She could tell she'd hit a sore point.

"I like your idea," she said. "It sounds more…sophisticated."

Less like a singles bar, she wanted to say. He wouldn't remain single a week in that atmosphere, she'd bet a pound of artichoke hearts on that.

"There are a lot of restaurants in Boston. Most of the new ones don't last very long. It's hard to build a name for yourself quickly. Not like up here, say, where there isn't all that much competition and overhead is low, so you can take time to build a reputation."

Julia could see how that would be true. Even her own business, real estate, was less competitive up in Blue Lake. There just weren't as many people out there, doing the same thing.

"There's something to be said for living out here in the country, you mean?" she teased him.

"Exactly. I grew up in Dorset," he said, mentioning a town not too far away. "My dad still lives there."

Dorset, huh? No wonder she'd never run into him. Just on the other side of the mountain. Different high schools. He must have been a few years ahead of her, she guessed. Four or five. That kind of age spread mattered a lot when you were a teenager.

Though it was ideal now, she thought vaguely. Most men didn't really start to settle down or think seriously about having children until they were at least thirty-five. At least that's what she'd found.

"Every time I come back for a visit, it looks pretty good to me," he added.

"Maybe for a weekend. But you'd get bored if you ever had to move back up here."

"I'm not so sure. Not that I don't enjoy the city. But maybe I'm getting to the 'been there, done that' stage." He looked over at her with a thoughtful expression. "What's kept you here so long, Julia? If you don't mind my asking. You seem like the girl voted most likely to succeed."

The compliment softened the implication a bit. She did mind him asking. Though the question was fair enough. "Pretty sharp...for a country girl, you mean?"

He laughed. "That's not exactly what I meant, but...you're not answering my question."

"Well...I went away to college. University of Pennsylvania," she added. "I liked Philadelphia. But I came back after graduation to marry a guy I grew up with, who wanted to take a job in his family's business. At least until we got established." She paused and pushed a bit of rice around her dish with her fork.

"We divorced eventually. And I did think of leaving here.

Even scouted out different cities, applied for jobs. But by then, I had the real-estate business established and it seemed foolish to just pick and start over some place new. And I didn't really want to leave Lucy," she added. "I'm pretty much all she's got."

"You're an only child?" Julia nodded. "I'm the baby of the family," he told her with a grin. "I have an older sister and brother. Our mother died when I was ten. It was hard on my dad."

And hard on a ten-year-old little boy, she imagined, feeling sorry for him. She could picture him back then; a thick, dark mop of hair, all arms and legs.

"Where are you sister and brother? Do they live around here?"

"Both left Vermont. My brother hates the cold. He ended up in Tucson. He's a college professor there. My sister is a lawyer. She lives in Connecticut. I'm the closest to Lester. I wouldn't want to move too far away from him. It's good of you to think of your mother," he added.

"Thanks," she said simply.

He did seem to understand and didn't seem to be judging her, or deciding she was timid, or lacked ambition or some attractive, adventurous streak by choosing to stay in such a small town.

"When I was younger I thought I was totally in control of my destiny," Sam confided. "Everything that happened to me—or didn't—was my decision. My will. I thought. But now, I don't think that's really true. I think sometimes we can't control what happens to us. Where we land on the game board. What we end up doing for a living. Falling in love. Or out of it… All those things. So much is just chance. Or maybe just meant to be."

Was he talking about himself? His past marriage? Or was he thinking more about Lester and Lucy now? It was hard to tell.

Julia wasn't sure how their conversation had taken such a philosophical turn. One minute, she was complimenting the im-promptu paella, and now they were discussing fate and destiny.

"I don't believe in destiny," she said finally. "That a person is fated to bump their fender in a parking lot on a certain day and time. Or win the lottery. Or meet a certain other person…" She stopped herself, fearing she'd revealed too much of her own secret frustrations.

"I just don't believe in that stuff." She smiled and shrugged. "I think we all make our choices and have to take responsibility for them."

He nodded, looking a bit amused. "I could have guessed you'd say that."

Julia felt self-conscious. So, the slate wasn't entirely clear, was it? He still seemed to think she was an uptight type, disagreeing with his romantic world view. He hadn't said it, of course, but she could tell what he was thinking.

"Would you like some coffee? I can make cappuccino or espresso. I have this neat machine," she offered.

"Some espresso would hit the spot, thanks."

"Coming right up." She picked up her plate and then his, and carried both to the sink.

Now that they were done with the meal, she felt moved by a sudden need to have him out of the house, the sooner the better. Their conversation had gotten very personal and intimate very quickly. She wasn't used to opening up so easily with a man. She wasn't sure she liked it.

"I can help you with the dishes." He'd carried the empty platter to the sink and suddenly stood very close behind her.

Trying to get closer to the sink? Or just to her?

Julia felt the heat of his body and knew if she took one step backward, she'd be plastered up against him. Again.

"That's…okay," she said quickly, her voice a bit high-pitched. She grabbed the platter from his hand and set it in the sink. "I'm just going to stack for now. I'll take care of it later. Why don't you just relax and I'll get the coffee going?"

"Okay…sure."

He stepped away and walked into the family room. She

sagged against the sink, clutching the counter edge for support. Close call. She had to watch herself. Unlike Sam, she did believe she had control over her choices and her life…and her body parts.

Sam Baxter was definitely testing the system.

She poured water into the coffeemaker, took out the little premeasured packets and pushed all the necessary buttons. While steaming espresso shot out of the machine, she set out two demitasse cups on a tray with a sugar bowl and even managed to remember the tiny curls of lemon peel on the saucer, the way it was served in authentic Italian restaurants.

Not that she was trying to impress him or anything…

In the back of the cracker closet, she found some expensive-looking cookies a client had given her for Christmas, still sealed in a fancy tin. She set a few on a china plate and added it to the tray. Luckily she hadn't brought the cookies over to the food bank with the rest of the edible holiday gifts.

When she came out to the family room, she saw Sam crouched by the fireplace. He'd stacked on some logs and was stirring up the glowing embers, making the flames flare up, bright and full.

He turned to her and smiled. Then sat on the floor near the fire, his long jean-clad legs stretched out in front of him. "This is a very comfortable room. In a very pretty house. Have you lived here long?"

"About three years. I bought it after my divorce." She brought over the tray and set it on the coffee table. "It was a total wreck. But I needed a bargain. Like most people, I was overly optimistic about the speed and cost of fixing it up."

"You did a great job. It's like something out of a magazine. All the furniture is very interesting, too."

"I found a lot here, and had some of the nicer pieces refinished. It all sort of goes together. At least, I think so." Julia smiled.

"It goes together nicely. You have a good eye."

"Thanks…but don't look too close. There's still a lot to do. But you can work on an old house like this forever. They never quite get finished."

"Maybe that's the fun, what attracts people to start in the first place."

"Maybe. From what I've seen it's mostly couples who jump in headfirst. Without any idea of the headaches. It either brings them closer…or they end up in divorce court," she added, making him laugh.

"A lot like couples who open a restaurant together," he observed. "You can tell a lot about their relationship by watching them in the kitchen when they think no one is around."

What did he think after cooking with her? They'd worked without any arguments. But it was basically him cooking and her working hard to keep her distance.

Maybe that said it all right there.

He leaned over, added a spoonful of sugar to his coffee and took a sip, then gazed up at her. "Aren't you going to sit down?"

"Sure…of course." She felt awkward, but was still figuring out her options.

She didn't really want to sit with him on the floor. That might give him the wrong idea. But if she took a seat up on the couch, that would look…odd. As if she was waiting for an appointment with the dentist. Or afraid of him. Or shy around men or something.

Or…the U-word again. Uptight.

Finally, she sat on the floor, too. With long legs stretched out straight in front and her back ramrod straight, leaning against the couch.

He reached over to the tray and picked out a rolled cookie filled with chocolate cream. Watching him consume it in three small bites was an education in sensuality.

"Hmm. Wafer cookies. My favorite."

Hers, too. Though she didn't confide it.

Julia took her coffee cup from the tray and added the lemon peel twist. He took another cookie, a look of pure pleasure registering on his handsome features.

It was starting to unnerve her.

"So…how long will you be visiting your father? Just the weekend?"

I hope.

"My plans are sort of flexible. Lester is talking about getting married this week at a justice of the peace. I'll certainly stay around for that."

Julia gulped and struggled to hide her dismay. Justice of the peace? She hadn't heard any of that. Of course, she'd never bothered to call her mother back today at work, either. And when she did call from her cell on the way home, her mother wasn't home.

This was a perfect opening for another knock-down, drag-out argument. She struggled to resist the temptation. For some reason she didn't want to examine too closely, she didn't feel the least bit like arguing with him again. Everything felt so peaceful and easy between them tonight. She didn't want to spoil it.

"I guess we'll have to see if the wedding plans come together that quickly. My mother usually can't decide what color to polish her nails in that time frame."

"Yes, we'll have to wait and see." He laughed. His smile was totally disarming. "Why do you ask? Looking to get rid of me?"

"I was just wondering. I'd think you'd be under a lot of pressure right now, setting up a new business."

"We haven't settled on our location yet, so there's not too much I can do before that."

Too bad for her. She was hoping he'd be going back to Boston tomorrow.

He stretched out on his side, one arm folded, his cheek resting on his hand. The long, lean, relaxed length of him set her pulse racing.

Julia decided she didn't need the black coffee after all. She hoped he'd decide to leave after he finished his. But he looked far too comfortable now to be even thinking of leaving anytime soon.

She set her coffee cup on the table and glanced at her watch. "Wow, look at the time. I can't believe how late it is. I do have to work tomorrow," she added.

"Of course. I understand." He put down his coffee cup and sat up, facing her. "It's been great getting to know you, Julia. I had a wonderful time tonight."

He met her gaze and it was hard to look away. Julia tried without success.

"So did I," she said quietly. She felt her resolve starting to melt. If he moved closer, she knew it would be hard to move away.

She suddenly stood up, surprising him. She rubbed the bottom of her back, feigning an ache. "My back. It bothers me sometimes when I sit on the floor too long."

"Oh…right." He stood up, standing very close. She tried to put some space between them but felt the back of her legs touching the couch. "Sorry if I've kept you up too late."

She sighed. What an apology. In the best of all possible worlds, he could keep her up all night. No complaints.

But this was the real world. With real limitations and consequences. He had to leave. And she had to go up to her bed.

Alone.

"Well. Thanks again for making dinner." She struggled to dampen the nervous edge in her voice, but her words came out in a rush. "It was great."

"Thanks for inviting me to stay."

She hadn't really invited him. He'd invited himself. But it wasn't worth arguing the point. She could barely think. Barely breathe. With him standing so close to her now.

She tipped her head back to look up at him. She met his gaze, then looked down again.

She wracked her mind for some clever line that would gently

give him a hint and get him moving out the front door. But she could only come up with more small talk.

"We never got a chance to talk about Lester and Lucy," she realized.

"Not get into another argument, you mean?" He lifted her chin with his fingertip, so that she was looking into his eyes again. And couldn't look away.

And didn't want to.

"I'd rather not argue with you, Julia. In fact, I think I'm done talking all together...."

## Chapter Four

Before Julia could say a word more, he pulled her close, one hand cupping her cheek, the other cupping her bottom. Not that she tried that hard to resist him, she had to admit.

She felt as if she just...couldn't. Her body melted against his like a pat of butter on a slice of hot French bread. She felt as if she didn't have a chance. Didn't have a choice.

His mouth covered hers, tenderly at first, tasting and teasing her. Coaxing a response. As she sighed and kissed him back, the intensity of his touch grew.

Just as she'd imagined, his kiss wasn't in the least bit tentative or questioning. His embrace was bold, confident...and creative. Some distant part of her mind registered all this. Her trusted analytical powers were shut down, short-circuited. Fuses blown.

Sam Baxter had definitely short-circuited the system.

"Julia...you're so beautiful. You take my breath away." He unfastened the clip in her hair and spread her long golden locks with his hands, his mouth wandering along the curve of her neck. His voice was low and raspy, and Julia felt as if every nerve ending in her body had been rubbed with rough velvet.

Then he pulled his head back and cupped her face with his hands. He stared down at her and sighed, his dark eyes growing smoky, wandering hungrily over her features. His gaze telegraphed one clear message—he wanted her. Wanted her very badly.

She knew in a flash of instinct, she wanted him, too, and when his hand moved up and pulled down the zipper of her velvet hooded top, she didn't resist. His mouth dropped to the soft skin at the top of her breasts, bared by her low-cut bra. Her breath caught at the back of her throat as his lips and tongue wandered over the sheer fabric, tantalizing the tip of each throbbing breast. She felt the heat of his palms on her skin, gripping her waist and pulling her hips closer to his.

Julia told herself to pull away. Step back, while she still had a chance.

But she was mesmerized by the amazing sensations elicited by his mouth and tongue and hands. She pulled away for an instant and he stared down at her, an unspoken question in his eyes. She knew if at that moment, she pulled away completely, he would go. There would be no argument.

Her gaze dropped to his lips, and she felt herself weaken with longing. Her soft sigh seemed to push him over the edge. His head dropped and their lips met. It felt as if a bolt of lightning arced between them. Sam's mouth moved over hers hungrily and Julia gave herself over to the wonderful pressure of his warm, firm lips on hers. His touch was commanding, confident. He urged her to follow and she eagerly responded. Her mouth opened against his like a flower and their tongues met in an intimate dance.

Julia hardly knew herself, her hands slipping under his soft sweater and pushing it over his head. Her touch wandered from his broad shoulders to his muscular back, her entire body rising into his embrace, yearning to feel more of his warm, strong body molded to her own.

Sam had already slipped the velvet top down her arms and unfastened her bra. She was bare to his gaze, but felt strangely unself-conscious. She'd never felt so free and natural with any man. So totally, sensually in synch.

"Julia...lay down with me." He murmured the invitation against her bare skin, telegraphing a tingling sensation to every trembling limb.

He didn't need to say another word. They stretched out together on the soft rug in front of the fire. Julia quickly slipped off her pants and then unfastened the clasp on Sam's jeans. Then he lay still, practically holding his breath as she pulled the zipper down and slid the denim fabric down, stroking and caressing him. Her hands roamed hungrily over his body, stroking his long hard thighs and the hard ridge of his manhood that bulged beneath his shorts.

She tugged down his shorts and slipped them off his legs. She stroked and teased him, driving him to the edge, and felt a certain female power as she heard him groan with satisfaction at her touch. She felt her body respond, growing warmer and wilder within.

Sam gently pulled her down toward him and pressed his hot mouth to her breasts. First one, then the other. Her nipples had hardened to aching points and the touch of his lips felt electric. A hot molten wave of pleasure swept through her body. She clutched his head, aching to feel more of his caresses.

"You're beautiful. I can't believe how beautiful you really are," he whispered.

Julia's mind was lost in a sensuous haze as his hands stroked and caressed her, his fingers outlining the graceful curve of her thigh, then dipping into the warm, honeyed center of her womanhood.

He sighed against her mouth, then kissed her deeply, all the while gliding his fingers inside and outside of her. Wave upon wave of hot pleasure broke over her body.

Breathless and aroused to a fevered pitch, she felt about to explode.

Julia was no prude. She enjoyed making love, giving and receiving pleasure. But she'd never responded like this. This was different. It was almost as if everything else had been a prelude. A practice drill. This was the real game. The World Series. She'd never been so in tune with a man, so perfectly matched in a dance of pure pleasure. Effortlessly. Wordlessly. As if he could intuit just what she was feeling and thinking. What she needed. What she craved.

Sam moved over her and she guided him, with her hands on his slim hips, urging him to move inside of her. She lifted her head and pressed her lips to his chest, her tongue swirling around one flat male nipple. She felt him react, and heard him groan with delight. She fitted herself even closer, eager to feel him sink into her velvety heat.

Then she moved with him as he thrust himself inside of her. Unbearable pleasure shook her body, wave upon wave breaking over. She could barely stand it any longer and never wanted it to end.

Finally, she trembled and shook as brilliant lights exploded behind her eyes, reaching pleasure's peak. Her head dropped limply back against the floor and she gasped for air.

Sam's mouth dipped down to her breast, his tongue twirling around her sensitive nipple. "I'm just getting warmed up, gorgeous," he whispered.

He slowly rocked inside of her, teasing and tempting, until she felt herself rising again to another astounding peak.

She moaned and held him tight, his hips arching up as he thrust deep inside of her. Julia closed her eyes and wrapped her slim legs even tighter around his waist. She matched his movements, rocking in an ageless, sensual dance. Higher still, until she felt herself shatter into tiny, sparkling fragments. Like a crystal, shattered. Like stars exploding in a velvet blue sky. At the very same moment, she felt Sam reach his own peak. He trembled for a long moment, then collapsed into her arms.

They lay together without saying a word. Sam's damp cheek

rested next to hers. He lifted his head and kissed her hair. Finally, he stared down at her. He slowly smiled.

"I guess we've stopped arguing."

Julia tilted her head to one side on the pillow. "It would seem so. For now anyway," she teased him.

"Oh, I think I know how to deal with you now," he said. The dark light in his eyes challenged her. But she had to admit, she felt too relaxed and completely satisfied to reply.


Julia woke slowly the next morning, feeling snugly and re-laxed and...definitely not alone. She felt Sam's heavy arm curled around her waist, his chin nestled in her hair. So, it was true. It hadn't been just a fantastically pleasant dream after all. She slipped out of bed and grabbed a robe to cover herself. He looked as if he might wake up for a moment, then rolled to his back and sighed in his sleep.

She stood staring at him for a moment. He was perfectly gor-geous, the comforter twisted around his lean hips, his muscular, hair-covered chest rising and falling with deep breaths. His thick dark hair, thoroughly but attractively mussed on the pillow, his rugged features relaxed in sleep.

She liked the way he looked in her bed and had the urge to touch his hair and stroke his scruffy cheek. To kiss his eyes and his lips. To crawl back under the covers with him and make love all over again. Judging from last night, it wouldn't take much to wake him. Especially certain parts of his anatomy.

She valiantly squelched the impulse.

In broad daylight, you should have a little control over your-self, a chiding voice reminded her.

Unlike last night, when all he had to do was grab her and kiss her and she melted into a panting puddle of lust.

Julia sighed and slipped into the bathroom. She took a quick shower, then collected her clothes and dressed in the guest room.

Down in the kitchen, she started a pot of coffee, then surveyed the mess that was left over from last night. The aftermath of a lovely party. The damning evidence of her demise.

When the house was a mess, she couldn't think straight. But she still made no move to start cleaning up.

It was hard to think straight this morning, period. How had this happened anyway?

One minute, she was yelling at the man like a lunatic in the middle of Main Street. A few hours later, she was rolling around on the floor with him, too eager to make the short trip upstairs to the bed.

She'd had her share of encounters with men. She'd even been wildly attracted to a few. But never like this. She'd never experienced anything like it. She'd never been so…impulsive before. Or given in so easily to her sensual side. Last night had been a once-in-a-lifetime plunge. Like…sky diving. Or a bungee jump?

She'd just shut off her brain—the practical, analytical part—and let the urging of her body and heart lead her.

She had to admit, she'd felt so free. Weightless. This morning she felt the weight of the world fall back on her shoulders again with a mighty, silent thump.

She poured herself a mug of coffee and took a sobering sip. How could she have gone to bed with Sam Baxter? What a stupid thing to do. What a ridiculous mistake.

She'd gone from euphoria to sheer dread. How was she going to face him? What would she say?

He had to think she was the easiest, most indiscriminating woman in Vermont. On the entire eastern seaboard, probably. When he woke up, that was, and started thinking about it.

And when would that be? She checked the kitchen clock. It was only seven-fifteen. Julia woke up early, no matter what. It was just her metabolism. She'd always been that way and her father used to call her the human alarm clock when she was growing up. During the week, it gave her time to exercise, catch up with house-work and read the newspaper before she headed into town.

She guessed Sam was the type who slept late, especially on a Sunday. After last night's performance, the man deserved some rest.

She knew leaving the house while he was still asleep was the coward's way out, but once the idea occurred to her, it seemed the only way out of the awkward mess.

Besides, he probably jumped into bed with women he hardly knew all the time. She'd heard stories about the restaurant business. It sounded pretty wild. A real party atmosphere. He seemed like a man who didn't mind enjoying himself. Indulging in all life had to offer. And, he was impossibly attractive. Women were probably throwing themselves at him all the time. She felt a twinge of jealousy considering that fact, though she knew she had no right. He'd acted last night as if it was something special, but he'd probably be relieved if she played it cool.

Face it, Julia. You're just another notch on Chef Sam's chopping block. When she thought of it that way, sneaking out didn't seem so awful. Maybe she'd be making it easier for him, too.

Julia grabbed a big yellow pad that she kept by the telephone and scrawled a quick note:

*Dear Sam,* she began. Then she ripped off the page and crunched it in a ball.

*Sam—* she started again on a less personal note. *Had to get to the office early today. Help yourself to coffee. The front door will lock automatically when you leave.*

She stood there a moment, chewing on the end of the pen and wondering what else to say. Wild possibilities raced through her brain….

*Thanks for a spectacular night. When I asked you to stay I had no intention of things going so far. But, just like your cooking, I couldn't resist. Your lovemaking was even better than dinner…if possible…*

Get a grip, Julia.

She sighed and took another sip of coffee. Of course she wouldn't write any of those things.

First of all, she didn't have the nerve to be so honest.

Julia thought she heard a sound upstairs and suddenly froze. She listened carefully, holding her breath.

Just the heating system, which sometimes rattled and wheezed on a cold morning. Her old house had its quirks. She hoped the noise hadn't woken Sam and took the cue to escape while she still could.

At the bottom of her short note she simply dashed off her name. Julia.

No "Love."

Or "Fondly."

Or even "Have a nice day!"

It wasn't going to be easy, but she'd made a big misstep with him last night. Now she had to backtrack. Pronto.

Julia arrived at Home Sweet Home Realty a short time later. And about two hours before she really needed to be there. She unlocked the door and went straight back to her office. She slipped off her coat and dropped her briefcase, immediately feeling better on her own turf, in her own orderly world where she was the boss. She felt her head clear of the craziness that had overtaken her—body and soul—last night in Sam Baxter's arms.

She did feel a pang of guilt about running out the way she had. It wasn't like her to run out on a man she'd spent the night with. Even if things hadn't worked out perfectly. Which was hardly the problem with Sam….

She pictured him still sleeping in her bed. A sizzling image of making love with him popped into her brain. Julia quickly doused it.

That kind of thinking would only soften her resolve.

They'd made a mistake. But he'd have to understand. By the time she spoke to him again, she'd be ready to explain in a calm, reasonable way.

She turned on her computer and readied her mind to start the workday. She had advertised a few houses in the classified section of weekend newspapers and Julia expected a busy day of calls and appointments.

With any luck, she wouldn't have time to think about Sam Baxter. Or if she'd made a second mistake by running out on him this morning.

At about nine-thirty, a few of the realty sales people wandered in. Julia didn't like to pressure her employees to work on Sunday, especially if they had families. Watching a kid's sports game or celebrating a family event was far more important than selling a house. Even she knew that. She tried to keep schedules flexible and let them decide on their own priorities. Most of the time the system worked out just fine.

This Sunday, like most others, Anita Engelmann and Tim Hatch were covering the office and calls.

Anita had been working for Julia for years. Her children were in college and her husband liked to ski in the winter and golf in the summer, so he barely noticed she was out of the house on Saturdays and Sundays. Anita was sharp and experienced, but still gave clients a "warm fuzzy feeling"—as if they were working with a beloved aunt or family friend.

Then there was Tim, a history teacher at the high school who sold real estate part-time and during the school break. Tim was probably going to open his own office once he retired, Julia guessed. He'd be good competition, too. But for now, he and Anita vied for the big sales at Home Sweet Home.

She always gave Marion Sundays and one other day during the week off. Julia usually didn't mind answering her own phone. But today she did. She didn't want to catch Sam on the other end of the line and have to start explaining herself.

Maybe he wouldn't call her. The sudden notion was stunning. She wasn't sure if she felt relieved…or upset, realizing it was possible.

A light on her phone flashed and Julia checked the number.

It was the main line and could possibly be Sam. That was the number he'd call.

Of course, it could also be any one of a hundred people who would call today to ask about the advertisements. When no one outside picked it up after a few rings, Julia cleared her throat and answered it. "Realty office. Can I help you?"

"Julia, it's me. Your mother."

Lucy always greeted her that way when she was upset. As if Julia could forget the sound of her own mother's voice.

"Hi, Mom. I called you back last night. You must have been out. Did you get my message?"

"I was out with Lester. Yes, I did get your message. So, you want to get together later, after work?"

"If you're not busy. Why don't we meet somewhere in town? I'll take you out to dinner."

"Oh…you don't have to do that…."

"I want to. Honestly. This way we can just sit and talk. No distractions."

Julia knew that unless her mother was trapped in a public place, she could devise a million clever ways to undermine and totally avoid a conversation. Her techniques ranged from jumping up to answer a telephone—that sometimes wasn't even ringing—to letting in her cat. Or letting the cat out again. Or running down to the basement in answer to some ominous sound from the washing machine. One that Julia never seemed to hear.

There were fewer opportunities at a restaurant, though the waiter could be summoned for strange reasons and running to the ladies' room was always an option.

Julia also thought she owed her mother a nice dinner out to make up for Friday night, when she'd probably delivered a few insensitive comments about Lucy's marriage plans and her mother's romantic track record in general after Lester and Sam had left.

Was that only two days ago? Julia sighed. It felt like a lifetime. What a difference a day makes….

"Well…okay. That would be nice. I suppose." Lucy still sounded hesitant. "But you have to promise you won't browbeat me about marrying Lester. He knows that you object to the match and he's very upset. His feelings are hurt."

Julia sighed. Now she had to worry about hurting Lester's feelings. Clever of him to play the role of the victim and draw on Lucy's sympathy.

"I won't browbeat you, Mother. Whatever that's supposed to mean. But I would like to talk about this situation a little more before you jump into anything. Think about me. I'd never even heard of Lester Baxter and then the doorbell rings…and you announce you're going to marry him. What about my feelings?"

Lucy sighed. "Yes…I understand. Lester does, too. That was inconsiderate of us to just spring it on you that way. I understand what you're saying…."

Was her mother going to remind her now of how she never liked surprises? Julia thought she would have to hit the hold button, and then let out a long scream.

"Why don't we just talk it through tonight, Mom? I promise I won't get upset."

"Okay, dear. I understand. I do want you to be happy for me and be on board with this whole thing. It's important to me…I love you."

Julia felt her heart soften. "I love you, too, Mom. Don't worry. It will all work out fine."

*I hope,* she added silently.

They made a plan to meet in town at the Stone Lion Inn. It was a little formal and old-fashioned for Julia's taste, but was her mother's favorite.

Julia hung up, feeling better about life in general. The situation with her mother had definitely upset her balance, her entire perspective. One reason she'd lost her mind and fallen into bed with Sam Baxter so easily. She just wasn't herself this weekend. Suffering from shock or something.

She turned in her chair to look out the open door of her private office. She saw Anita at her desk, going through listings on the computer with a young couple. Promising…

The front door opened and Rachel waved to her. Julia stood up and waved at her to come on back.

"You must have ESP. I am so ready for a break."

"Not really. I just stopped by to drop this off. I forgot to stop on my way home last night." Rachel dug into her huge purse and pulled out a copy of *Pride and Prejudice*.

"That's all right. I didn't have much time for reading last night anyway…." Julia glanced up at Rachel but didn't know where to begin. Her expression must have hinted that big news was on the way. Her friend gave her a questioning look.

"Really? Did you have an unexpected date?"

"You could call it that. Sam Baxter dropped by. You know, the hot-looking chef? Lester's son?"

"I remember. Go on." Julia saw a small smile begin to blossom on Rachel's pretty face.

"He wanted to apologize. After I ran into him at the general store, right after I saw you yesterday morning, we got into an argument about our parents. I said he was illogical and naive. He called me uptight and…close minded."

"Sounds nasty."

"Oh, it was… That's why it seemed so amazing that after all that he came over and ended up cooking dinner for us…."

Rachel held her hand up, like a traffic cop. "Wait a second. He cooked dinner, too?"

Julia nodded. "He stopped by to apologize and I had something in the oven that started to burn…. It's a long story. The thing is, after dinner, we were just hanging around, talking. And he was saying good-night and about to go. And somehow…he never left."

Rachel did not have any reaction for a long moment. Julia was afraid to imagine what her friend might be thinking. Then a huge smile lit up Rachel's face.

"Wow. That's great. He sounds pretty wonderful. I'm really happy for you."

Julia leaned forward and grasped Rachel's hand. "Rachel… You don't understand. I hardly know the guy. It wasn't even a real date, for goodness' sake. He just mixed up a bunch of left-overs in my fridge…." She paused and tried to compose herself. "The guy just kissed me. And I practically ripped his pants off. Like a sex-starved cave woman. It's…embarrassing."

"Oh, Jules. Calm down. You're just second-guessing yourself. Don't you ever read women's magazines? Men love that cave-woman routine. They don't always want to do all the dragging."

"Let's not joke about this. It isn't funny. I never act that way. Not with anybody."

"Yes, I know. Maybe it's time you did. Maybe it's a good thing. Don't you see? You're always so cautious and careful with the men you date. You have that rule about dating them a certain number of times before this or that can happen. You're always so objective, tallying their good points and their bad. As if they were baseball players, collecting a stat sheet. This guy blew the stat sheet right out the window. He just…swept you off your feet. I've never heard you say you were that attracted to anyone. Isn't that…good?"

Julia swallowed hard. What Rachel said was true. Sam had swept her off her feet. But it wasn't anything to be happy about.

"I am attracted to him. Wildly, if last night is any evidence. But…I just don't trust that. I don't even really know him. And besides, it could never work for the long term in a million years. We're just so different. You have no idea…."

"You keep saying that, Julia. But…" Rachel stopped herself. Julia had a feeling her friend didn't want to give too much advice. "How did you leave it with him? Did you make plans to see him later? Or call?"

Julia met her glance, then looked away. It was hard to admit her cowardly deed. But it felt like a relief to come clean with Rachel.

"I left the house while he was still asleep. I left him a note on the kitchen table. A real morning-after chicken…right?"

Rachel slowly nodded. "Definitely in the poultry category," she admitted. "Did he call you this morning?"

Julia shook her head. It was about half past ten. Was he possibly still sleeping and hadn't read the note yet?

She sighed and dropped her chin in her hand. "I just didn't know what to do."

Rachel patted her shoulder. "Don't worry. If you like him, just let him know how you feel. Why don't you just try to catch up with him? Call your house right now?"

Julia glanced at her, then looked at the phone. She could call and try to catch him having coffee. That would make things better.

Then she got cold feet. Chicken feet.

"I do like him. But I don't want to encourage anything. Last night was a total fluke."

Rachel didn't answer for a moment. She wasn't smiling anymore, Julia noticed.

"Well, even if you feel that way, you probably have to talk about it with him at some point. I mean, you can't just pretend it didn't happen. It's not as if you'll never see him again. If things work out with Lester and Lucy, I mean."

"That's true. Unfortunately. I'm meeting my mother tonight for dinner. So we can talk about Lester. She still sounds dead set on marrying him."

"See? You really can't brush this guy off so easily, Julia. Not like the others."

Rachel smiled, as if she was secretly happy about that part, Julia thought. Then she leaned over and gave Julia a hug. "I have to run. Don't worry. You can handle this. I know you'll say just the right thing."

Under most circumstances, that would be true. Julia prided herself on her social skills and always seemed to know how to say the right thing. Even in awkward situations like this one.

But something about Sam left her totally tongue-tied. Speechless. Her mind went blank.

Which was probably how she'd ended up going to bed with him last night. The simple words *No, thank you* had been erased from her vocabulary.

Julia heard a knock on the door and Anita peeked in. "The Watsons are here to see you," she said.

"Thanks. Please tell them I'll be right out."

The door closed again and she glanced at Rachel. "My ten o'clock appointment. Guess it's showtime."

"Do you have a lot of appointments today?"

"Enough to keep me busy."

Julia had a few houses lined up to show Sue and Jeff Watson, who had been looking a few months for a country place. The Watsons were nice, but what she'd call "real lookers," unable to agree on what they liked or make a commitment. She had a feeling they were starting to see other Realtors in the area, like Archie Newland, her main competition. After all the time she'd put in she hoped one of her properties would click for them.

After the Watsons, she was scheduled to meet with a seller for a possible new listing. It was a plum and she hoped she could sign him on. The schedule would keep her out of the office most of the day, which was just as well.

She didn't need any more sitting around here, daydreaming about last night. Bemoaning the fact that she'd made spectacular love to a terrific man...who she just couldn't get involved with.

She rose from her desk and fished in her handbag for a lip gloss. "Thanks for letting me vent, Ray."

"What are friends for?" Rachel rose and they walked out of the office together. "Keep me posted, okay?"

"You're the first person I'll call for backup," Julia promised. She smiled a goodbye, then turned to greet her clients as Rachel let herself out of the office.

"Hi, Sue. Hi, Jeff." Julia extended her hand in warm greeting.

"I have some really great properties to show you today. Three listings that just came on the market. Let's look at the specs before we go out."

She led the couple back to a worktable and showed them the photos and information about the listings. They seemed very excited and Julia had a feeling the Watsons—who were quite particular—would find the elusive dream home they'd been looking for.

Why was work so easy…and life so hard?

## Chapter Five

Julia called her office twice from the road during the day to check her messages. There weren't many, since it was Sunday. None at all from Sam.

A heavy feeling settled in her heart as twilight fell and she drove back to the village from her day of appointments. She mentally reviewed the short note she'd left on the kitchen table for him. Did it suggest, somewhere between the lines, a subtle "goodbye and good luck" message?

It had not been warm, fuzzy and effusive, that was for sure. But Julia didn't think her brief excuse for leaving the house early could be interpreted in a negative way. Not if a person was fair minded. Not enough to make that person angry or hurt...and never call you after spending a totally glorious night in your arms.

Could it?

She parked in front of the Stone Lion Inn, on the village green in town, suddenly realizing that, here she was all upset that he hadn't called her. Wasn't that what she'd wanted this morning?

She sighed and shut the car engine. To be perfectly honest with herself, when it came to Sam Baxter, she didn't know what she wanted.

Julia quickly checked her hair and lipstick in the rearview mirror, preparing herself for the last hurdle of the day: dinner with her mother. After that, she would go home, take a long hot bath and read her book group book. Last night's plan that had gone so unexpected astray.

The Stone Lion Inn was in a gracious Queen Anne Victorian on the village green. It was the best hotel in the area and quite crowded in the fall during the height of tourist season. The lobby was decorated in an opulent, turn-of-the-century style. Julia found her way through the large lobby, weaving a path around antique love seats and potted palms, where formal high tea was served in the late afternoon. A hostess greeted her at the entrance to the dining room, but Julia had already spotted her mother seated at a table by a window.

Lucy waved wildly, as if flagging a taxi in Times Square. Julia couldn't help but smile as she walked on over to meet her.

"Hello, Mom. Waiting long?" Julia quickly kissed Lucy's cheek, then took a seat across from her.

"Just a few minutes. Were you busy today in the office?"

"The office was pretty quiet, but I was out most of the day with clients. What were you up to?"

Lucy shrugged. "Oh…this and that. I took a ride with Lester. He saw some ads in the paper for farm properties so we went just to take a look."

Lester hadn't bought her mother an engagement ring yet, as he'd promised. Shouldn't that be first on their shopping list? Before the farm property?

She didn't point that out to her mother, careful not to start off on the wrong foot again.

Julia felt her jaw clench as she forced a normal tone of voice. "Really? See anything interesting?"

"What do I know about farms? They all looked pretty much the same to me. Though one of the houses looked awfully run-down. I didn't even want to go inside."

"Those old farm houses can be pretty nasty. Spiders, mice... bats in the attic. You'd be surprised."

Her mother shivered, looked suitably creeped out. Julia hid a grin. "I guess so. I never thought of that," Lucy admitted.

Julia picked up a roll from the basket on the table, then put it down again. Perhaps it wasn't fair to scare her mother that way. But she was telling the absolute truth. Her mother had a right to know the whole story before she signed on as Mrs. Lester Baxter, Farm Wife.

"Sam went inside with Lester. He didn't seem put off. He seems to know something about buying property, too. I'm sure he'll be a big help."

Sam was there? Julia felt a jolt. So he'd been out shopping for goat farms with his father all day and couldn't find a minute to call her? Well, some people have their priorities, don't they?

It was some relief to learn he hadn't just picked up and gone back to Boston—one possibility that had run through her brain.

"I know a little about real estate," Julia offered mildly. "Not that I'm dying to get involved in this..." She was going to say *scheme*. But that sounded too negative. "This plan," she said instead. "Not until I know a little more about Lester, anyway."

"Well, might as well get it all out on the table. So, you want to talk about Lester and our engagement. Okay, let's talk," Lucy declared. "We're in love. We want to get married and have a life together. For as long as we have left, anyway. What else do you want to know, Julia?"

Her mother's words were softly and gracefully spoken. But a challenge hung in the air. The gauntlet had been thrown and Julia could practically hear the romantic violins in the background of her mother's tender speech.

Or was that real violins? Julia turned to see a strolling player come toward them.

Just her luck. The background music certainly wasn't helping her side.

"Okay, Mom. Since you asked. What do you really know about him? Lester seems very nice, but you've only known him for a short time. Three or so weeks?"

"Three and half," her mother corrected.

"Okay, let's call it an even four. That's not very long, though. And it sounds as if you have no mutual acquaintances who know him, either. Isn't that right?"

"Eleanor Weeks has known him for years," Lucy corrected her, referring to her next-door neighbor. "She's the one who gave me his number."

"To fix the garbage disposal. But she doesn't know him socially. You know that's not what I mean."

Her mother looked down at the table, pouting. "Well, what of it? Do you think I need to have a private investigator check up on him?" Lucy nearly laughed.

Julia could tell her mother thought the very idea was ridiculous. Meanwhile, Julia had planned to take care of a background check on the Internet herself and would have started it last night, if she hadn't been sidetracked. It was quite simple to do these days. All you needed was the person's name and current address. The results came in a few days. Or it could be a rush order if necessary. It didn't cost much, either.

"Background checks are done all the time, Mother. In this day and age, you can't be too sure. It's smart and safe. Dating services and employment agencies do it all the time to screen out the undesirable types. People with criminal records. Con men…"

"I get your point, Julia," Lucy interrupted her. "I've never asked Lester if he's ever been arrested or been involved in any bogus business deals. But I'd bet my flat hat he hasn't," Lucy challenged.

Fire flashed in Lucy's blue eyes. She looked like a female tiger, defending her own. Julia already knew her mother was angry. But the truth had to be spoken. The cards had to be put out on the table, as Lucy had said. It was now or never.

"Mother, please. I'm just trying to look out for you. To protect you. I don't want you to do anything hasty that you'll end up regretting. I don't want to see you get hurt," she finished quietly.

Lucy's expression softened. "But I'd never regret marrying Lester. I just know it in my heart."

Lucy said this simply, as if the fact was as irrefutable as the sun rising in the west and setting in the east. It was that kind of romantic balderdash that Julia found so impossible to reason with.

Before she, too, could lose her temper, the waiter arrived. "Would you ladies like to hear the specials?" he asked politely.

"We would love that," Julia answered, grateful for the interruption.

The specials were recited and both Lucy and Julia ordered house salads and sea bass with saffron risotto.

"They make a nice chicken dish here. But I can have chicken anytime," Lucy remarked once the waiter left.

*Not the way I had it last night,* Julia wanted to say. But she held her tongue. She was dying to ask about Sam. Did he seem at all…unhappy? Moody? Quiet? As if he might have been thinking of her?

Of course, she didn't dare let her mother in on her secret. Thoughts of Sam did remind her of one important question she had to ask.

She waited until their salads arrived. Lucy had somehow changed the subject from Lester to a winter clearance sale at the local outlet mall. Julia wasn't sure how she'd managed it, but it was just one of her many evasion tactics in action.

"So maybe you'd like to come shopping with me one night next week. I'm sure there will be some great bargains," Lucy offered.

On wedding gowns, for instance? Julia nearly replied.

"Next week? Would that be before or after you and Lester visit a justice of the peace?"

Lucy's mouth hung open, a fork full of mixed greens dangling in the air. "Who told you that?"

"Sam—Sam Baxter did," Julia stuttered.

"Oh? When did you see him?"

"Um…let's see…" Julia struggled with her reply. She couldn't admit that she'd seen him last night. But it had to be some answer that would hold up if Lucy compared notes with Lester.

What had Sam had told his father about her? she suddenly wondered. And what would Lester tell her mother? Did Sam tell Lester why he hadn't come home last night?

"I guess we met up at the general store," she said finally. "Saturday morning. He walked with me down to the office. We had a long…chat."

"I see. Well, a justice of the peace was just a thought. Of course I was going to tell you if we decided to go through with it," Lucy added.

She definitely looked embarrassed to have the plan revealed and Julia wondered if her mother would have told her. Or just eloped.

Julia met her mother's gaze. "I hope so, Mom. I hope you wouldn't just run off and do something crazy."

Lucy set down her fork, looking frustrated. "See, there you go again. Why is it so crazy for me to marry Lester? I just don't understand what you have against him. Why, you've only met the man once."

Julia took a deep breath. It wouldn't do now to lose her temper, as she had on Friday night. But for the life of her, Julia didn't understand how her mother could possibly miss her meaning. More likely, she didn't want to understand. Or face it.

"That's just my point, Mom. I'd like to get to know him a little better before you marry him…. I think you should, too." She reached over and covered her mother's hand with her own. "It takes a long time to get to know someone. There's always that wonderful infatuation phase, floating on air, when people are totally blind to the other person's flaws. Do you want to wake up one day—like next week maybe—and decide you made you a huge mistake? I'm not saying you shouldn't marry Lester. But how about just being engaged for a while? It's really very nice to be engaged. People throw parties for you and give you china and appliances…. It's fun," Julia said, trying to coax her.

"But, Julia. We're old. I don't need any more appliances. Anything can happen at our age. I don't want to wait six months. Or even three months…"

"How about…two months?" Julia bargained. "You can go to Paris on your honeymoon. April in Paris?" Julia hummed the old show tune. "Doesn't that sound nice?"

Her mother smiled faintly but wouldn't say one way or the other if she agreed. "Is that your only objection? That we haven't known each other long enough?"

Unfortunately, it was not. Julia's second and larger point was harder to put forward. But this was her chance and she had to speak up. Or forever hold her peace.

"Mother, you're a woman with considerable assets," Julia began. "You're quite comfortable financially."

"And I'm very grateful for that, too," Lucy said, nodding in agreement. "Some women alone have very little security. I've been very lucky. That way, at least."

"Yes, you have. And it's not just women. There are lots of men who reach their golden years and find they just don't have the nest egg they'd planned on. Funds to do things. To take trips. And all that…" She took a breath.

Her mother looked curious, not guessing yet what this was all adding up to. "Take Lester, for example. If he wasn't marrying you, would he have the resources to buy property and start up a new business? I don't think so," Julia added, answering for her. "I doubt he'd get a bank loan easily, either. Lucky for him you've come along into his life right now. It makes all his dreams possible, doesn't it?"

She left the question hanging between them, watching her mother's expression as she processed the insinuations.

"What are you saying? Do you honestly think Lester is marrying me for money? So we can buy the farm together? That's an awful thing to say about him, Julia. I'm surprised at you. That's an awful thing to even think about the poor man."

Julia was afraid her mother would react this way—Lucy's eyes were filling with tears. She leaned over and patted her mother's shoulder. "Mother, please. Can't we discuss this reasonably?"

"What's reasonable about accusing the man I love of marrying me just for my money? Can't you see how he feels about me? How we feel about each other?" Lucy was weeping openly now. She patted her mouth and tossed her napkin on the table.

Julia didn't know what to say. Perhaps she'd gone too far but she had to voice her suspicions. She had tried to be diplomatic about it but her mother had always been a sensitive flower. And quite dramatic.

"Honestly, Julia. Sometimes you're just like your father. No sense of romance. None at all…"

That stung. Her mother's ultimate insult, comparing her to her father.

*I do have a sense of romance,* she wanted to argue back, *I just don't have to wave it about like a flag every minute…and act like some opera diva in the grand finale.*

"Mother," she said tightly, summoning every shred of patience she could muster, "I'm worried about you. All I'm asking is that you take some precaution before you take this big step. You hardly know Lester and it's a big risk."

Julia knew she sounded as if she was advising a teenage daughter about birth control. But role reversal had always been the name of the game between herself and Lucy. Why should this situation be any different?

"I want you to get a prenuptial agreement," she said finally. "If Lester's intentions are honorable, as you believe, then he should have no problem with it. If he's more in love with your bank account than your beauty and charm, you'll find out."

Lucy made a face. As if she'd tasted something sour.

"I was afraid you'd tell me to do that, Julia. I can't ask Lester to sign one of those things. I'll hurt his feelings. I'll insult him."

"What about my feelings, Mother?" Julia asked honestly. "You've known Lester for three weeks. I'm your daughter. If you won't do it for yourself, do it just for me. Blame all of it on me if you want. Make me the bad guy. I don't care. I just wish you'd take my advice. I'm just trying to take care of you."

"Yes...I know that, dear." She gently shook her head, then sighed. "Is that what will satisfy you, Julia? A prenuptial agreement? Will that make you feel better about me marrying Lester?"

"Much better. Totally better. I have nothing against the man, honestly," she added. "I'm just worried about you. I want to know that if things don't work out, you won't be left alone with nothing. Is that too much to ask?"

Lucy glanced at Julia, then looked away. "Well, I can't promise anything. But I will speak to him about it. You know Lester really wants you to like him. He's not comfortable getting married if you're all in a snit. I'd feel the same way about his son, Sam. We want our children to be happy for us. And involved."

Julia sighed. Her mother obviously had no idea how involved she'd already gotten with Sam Baxter. Above and beyond the call of duty.

"What about Sam?" she couldn't help asking. "How did he seem today? Looking at the farms, I mean?" She picked at her vegetables with the tines of the fork, but didn't eat any.

"He seemed...fine. Very upbeat kind of person," Lucy added. "He's a very good-looking man, don't you think? I'm surprised he's single."

Upbeat? While she was dragging around, feeling so blue?

"Maybe he likes being single. Maybe he's not interested in a commitment right now," Julia said quickly.

Maybe he likes to run around, cooking impromptu gourmet dinners for any woman he meets, taking them to bed. Moving on to the next kitchen, the next bedroom…

"Lester says he's still hurt from his marriage breaking up. He's afraid to get involved again. From what Lester says, I'm sure he has his chances."

"I wouldn't doubt it," Julia agreed. Another diversion from the main topic. But she was the one who'd asked about Sam.

Lucy took out a tissue and patted under her eyes. Her tears had smudged her eye makeup and she tried to make some repairs. "Do I have raccoon eyes?" she whispered. "I hate that."

Julia shook her head. "Not at all, you look fine. Want some coffee or dessert?"

Lucy shook her head. "No, thanks. I think I'm fine. That was a very lovely meal, Julia. You really don't have to treat."

"I insist," Julia said, signaling for the check.

The Stone Lion Inn was the priciest restaurant in town. But if her mother actually got Lester to sign a prenup the meal would be well worth it.

Julia paid the check and walked Lucy out to her car, which was also parked in front of the inn. It wasn't very late, but Julia felt beat. Perhaps from being up most of last night and her long workday. And fretting over Sam.

"I'm glad we had this talk, Mother. Even though it was difficult. At least I was honest with you about my concerns. And you were honest with me about your feelings for Lester."

Lucy patted Julia's arm. "Yes, dear. Honesty is the best policy. And if you can't be honest, at least try to be nice. I taught you that," she reminded her.

"Yes, Mom. You did." Julia laughed. The phrase summed up her mother's philosophy of life in a nutshell. "I'll ask my attorney to call you tomorrow to explain the agreement and what it involves. Then you can talk to Lester, okay?"

Lucy let out a long breath. Julia guessed it wasn't going to be easy for her to follow through and wondered if it would really happen.

"Okay, dear. I'll try my best."

Lucy's promise did not give Julia an iron-clad feeling of relief. But at least her mother had come this far. It was definitely progress and more than she'd honestly expected.

When Julia got home she tried not to race to the answering machine but couldn't help herself. There were three messages— two from Rachel, and one from the Watsons, saying they were ready to make an offer on a sweet cottage that Julia had shown them today with a pond on the property and a beautiful view.

The news should have cheered her. Or at least given her a sense of relief that her persnickety clients had finally settled on something. But she felt only disappointment. Sam had not called.

As she turned to leave the kitchen she spotted the note she'd written to him, still sitting on the table. It was no longer propped up on the coffee mug. In fact, it was stained with the ring from someone's coffee cup, so she knew he had read it. She crumpled it up and tossed it in the trash.

Perhaps she should have woken him up? Brought him coffee in bed? Kissed him good morning…the way she'd really wanted to?

Too late now. What was done was done. Julia sighed and headed upstairs to a hot bath, good book and warm—but empty—bed.

It was hard waking up the next morning. She overslept, which rarely happened. She felt foggy-headed and tired. She knew she'd had a bad dream, but couldn't remember what it was about.

She showered and dressed quickly in an easy "no-brainer" outfit—a long, belted black sweater and black pants with a gray-blue T-shirt underneath. *No bold colors today, sorry, Mom. I'm just not in the mood.*

She pinned her wet hair back in a tight knot at the back of her head, and added hoop earrings. A quick swipe of lipstick was all the makeup she had time for.

Mondays were filled with catch-up phone calls and paperwork. She rarely met with clients or even left the office for that matter.

Julia sailed into the office, the last to arrive. Marion was busy at her keyboard and glanced up with a smile.

"Morning, Marion. Any messages?" she asked quickly.

"The Watsons called. Sounds like they finally found a house they like. Amen."

"Oh, right. The Watsons." Julia realized she'd never called them back last night. Usually, once clients were ready to make an offer she was all over them. "Anyone else?"

"I found a few calls on the machine from yesterday. I left the slips on your desk. I guess you were all pretty busy. No one even picked up the phone, for goodness' sake…."

Marion's tone suggested that without her around, the place had been falling apart.

"It's just not the same on Sundays without you, Marion," Julia agreed. She dashed into her office to check the slips.

More Watsons. Three from couples who were selling houses and wanted to know if there had been any interest from the Watsons. One from a client giving her a listing. Another from a lawyer about a closing agreement. Then finally, on the very bottom of the pile…

Sam Backman called. Please call back, the slip read. Then a cell number. Then a second message from later in the day—Sam Bicksley called. Please call back. Same cell phone number.

Marion thought of herself as efficient, but had never been very good at getting names straight. Julia knew that Sam Backman and Sam Bicksley were one and the same…Sam Baxter.

Her entire body sagged with relief and she flopped into her desk chair, still holding the message slips like a prize.

Why hadn't she called the office machine and checked the messages from home last night? Because she'd thought either Anita or Tim had been here yesterday, picking up the phone. She had called and checked in with both of them while she'd been driving around to appointments.

How could she guess her staff was so inefficient? It was a wonder the business did so well....

But she couldn't be annoyed at them. She felt too happy for that. She felt so much better, so much brighter. She suddenly remembered being about seven or eight years old, and sometimes feeling she just had to do a cartwheel, wherever she was walking along at the time. No matter what her mother or father said.

Julia had that very same feeling, like doing a cartwheel right across her office.

See, he wasn't the kind of guy who didn't even call the next day. He didn't seem that type at all when they were making love. Anything but.

The light flashed on her phone and Marion picked it up. "It's Sue Watson again," she called to Julia from just outside the door. "Want to speak to her?"

Julia shook her head. "Take a message, please. Tell her I'm not in yet."

Marion looked confused, but got back on the line.

Julia rose from her desk and shut the door, then picked up her phone and dialed Sam's cell number. It rang several times. She felt her stomach churning with nerves, and her mouth getting dry. She wasn't even sure what she would say.

Finally, his voice came on. A recording.

The sound of his voice got to her, making her even more nervous. Julia cleared her throat and listened for the beep.

"Hi, Sam. This is Julia. It's Monday morning, around ten. I just found your messages from yesterday. I was out all day with clients. Just getting back to you. Give me a call...if you get a chance."

She hung up. Then let out a long breath. Had she sounded too nervous? Too happy? Too...something?

Okay, the ball was in his court now. Even though she doubted the game should continue, it felt good to know he'd called.

It was hard to focus on work after that. Julia forced herself to come back to earth. Her day quickly filled with calls and e-mails demanding her attention. A closing date on one pending sale was changed by the bank and that required lots of calls and changes on documents.

She ate lunch at her desk and called Rachel. Julia was eager to report the pink message slips but Rachel was in the middle of putting Charlie down for a nap and had to call her back.

Pretty Baby was closed on Mondays. Though when Rachel had just started her business, she'd kept the store open seven days a week, now that she and Jack were married, she didn't have the same financial pressure and had lots more time to spend at home with Charlie.

Julia sometimes wondered how much time she would have to spend with a baby, if she ever tried the single-mother route. Following Rachel's example, she imagined bringing her baby to the office every day and making a little nursery in some unused space. But having a baby in her office didn't seem as simple as Rachel's arrangement. Julia had to come and go so much. She wasn't sure it would work.

No need to worry about that right now, she reminded herself. She wasn't even pregnant and had no possibilities on the horizon. There was Sam, of course…but she hadn't gone to bed with him just to get knocked up. They'd used protection and the thought hadn't even crossed her mind.

Well, once or twice maybe, she had thought they could make some nice-looking children together. And he did seem very nurturing at times. As if he'd make a good father.

By the time Rachel called her back, Julia was too busy to chat. When she finally got up from her desk to stretch her legs and make a cup of tea in the office kitchen, she noticed it was nearly five. Marion was clearing off her desk, stacking mail to drop at the post office.

"Need anything before I go?" her assistant asked.

"No. Thanks. See you tomorrow, Marion."

"Right. See you. Don't work too late, Julia," Marion added.

"I won't." Julia sipped her tea and watched her go. Marion was like a second mother at times. Though much more sensible than Lucy. Giving a thought to her mother, Julia wondered why she hadn't heard anything from Lucy today. Their dinner conversation had been a heavy one. She was probably still digesting it.

Julia did feel a bit tired and considered going home. But Sam hadn't called back yet and she'd stupidly given him the office number. She could call back and leave her home and cell phone…and look totally desperate and needy…and obsessive.

Or just wait around a few minutes longer to see if he called back?

Julia decided to wait. She liked to check the listings on competitors' Web sites and hadn't had a chance to catch up on that today.

She was focused on that task, staring at her computer screen, when she sensed someone standing in her office doorway. She assumed it was Anita, stopping by to say good-night. Then she heard the sound of a deep throat clearing and knew it was not Anita.

She looked up, startled at the sound.

It was Sam.

He stood with his hands in the pockets of his leather jacket. His dark eyes fixed on her, his expression thoughtful.

"The door was open and no one was out there, so I just walked in. I didn't mean to scare you."

"That's okay." Julia sat back in her chair. "I called you this morning. Did you get my message?"

"Yes, I did. And you got mine."

"Just this morning. I was out all day with clients. Nobody told me that you'd called here."

"I see."

He walked into her office, but didn't sit down.

This wasn't quite the way she imagined it would be, seeing him again. She imagined at least a smile. Maybe a hug or tiny kiss hello?

He seemed so…distant.

She stood up and walked around her desk. "Would you like to sit down?"

There was a sofa and two chairs on the other side of her office. He glanced that way, but shook his head. "No…thanks. I can't stay long."

The tone in his voice made her nervous.

"I'm sorry I had to go so early on Sunday morning. I had to get over here and open up. I had an appointment to prepare for," she elaborated.

He nodded. "I understand…. I just wondered if there was something I did that made you upset? Or annoyed?"

Julia was shocked by the question. It was the one she should have been asking him. She shook her head. "No…not at all."

You did everything right, pal. Believe me, she wanted to assure him.

"I like you," she blurted out. He stared at her, his expression softening a bit, his eyes brighter.

"I like you, too." He looked confused but amused at her confession. "I thought that was…apparent."

She smiled. She couldn't help herself. Then she looked away.

"I just think it's unfortunate that it's such bad timing. I mean, the night we spent together was just great. It was…"

"Awesome? Wonderful? Perfect?" he finished for her.

She sighed and nodded. "Absolutely."

"But?" He crossed his arms over his chest, looking concerned. Bracing himself for what she was going to say next.

She swallowed hard and looked away again. "But…I don't think it was such a great idea to go to bed with you. I mean…it's gotten very complicated, with our parents and all. And you're starting a new business all the way in Boston and I'm here…. I can't see how we'd ever have time to see each. I can't see how it would ever work out."

"Blue Lake isn't that far from Boston, Julia. You make it sound like you live on the moon."

"I know, but…" She sighed and paced around in front of him. "Look, I'm not the type of person who just jumps into bed with a man. On a first date…or whatever that was. That never happens with me."

He looked pleased to hear it. "I sort of had that impression."

"But one night is one night and I can't see how this would work in the long run. We're obviously very different. We think differently. We want different things out of life right now. I'm not in the market for a…" Meaningless affair, she nearly said aloud. "A lovely but pointless fling with a guy who lives six hours away."

"At least you think I'm lovely." He forced a smile, but she could tell she'd hurt his feelings. "I don't like the pointless part though," he added. "And why do you have to worry so much about the long run? How about just the short run? How about taking it day by day?"

He did have a good point. She did tend to worry too much. To prepare herself for problems that might never happen. But this was different. She knew it wouldn't work. And now, after seeing him again face-to-face, she knew it would just hurt so much when it ended. More than it did now.

"Sam…don't you understand? Just a little?"

He sighed, but didn't answer. "What about our parents?" she continued. "Doesn't that make it complicated for you, too?"

"I can't argue you with about that. It's getting messier by the minute. They went out today to shop for a ring, and your mother asked my father to sign a prenuptial agreement. She said it was your idea and she wants to put your mind at ease."

The tone of his voice didn't bode well. "And…how did it go? What did your dad say?"

"What do you think he said? He was crushed. He called the whole thing off. Now they're both miserable."

"And everyone blames me?"

His expression looked sympathetic, but just for a moment. "Well…yes."

"Do you blame me?" she asked quietly. "I mean, I only did it because I'm worried about my mother. I didn't expect it to be a…deal breaker."

Sam sighed. He looked as if he might reach out to comfort her and her entire body craved his touch. It was all she could not to sway toward him.

"I think I am getting to know you a little, Julia. The way you think. I know you had good intentions. But you just can't help yourself. You're the type of person who buys a lot of insurance policies, preparing for any possible disaster. But that's not always the way life works out. Sometimes there are no guarantees. Sometimes you just get struck by lightning. No matter what you do. Sometimes, you just have to go with your gut, trust your intuition, know what I mean?"

She nodded sadly. "I suppose that works for some people. It's just not my style. I'm the type who buys a lightning umbrella," she admitted.

He smiled slowly. "Then I guess I really am the exception. What was it exactly that swept you off your feet? My new aftershave?"

"Your cooking, I think," she said quietly, teasing him back.

"Of course. Works like a charm every time."

Every time, huh? Julia felt stung. So she was just another notch on his chopping block after all.

"So…what now?" she asked, quickly changing the subject back to Lester and Lucy. "No wedding at a justice of the peace this week, I guess."

"That plan is off. I'm heading back to Boston. I can always run back in time if they patch it up."

Julia felt a pang in her heart. So, he was leaving town. He'd come to say goodbye, not to persuade her to continue their relationship.

"They'll patch it up." She forced a note of optimism she truly didn't feel.

And what about us? Was he giving in so easily? He wasn't going to try any harder to talk her into seeing him, she realized.

For one thing, he had too much pride. For another, he probably had his choice of women, more convenient and welcoming of his attentions, than a conflicted, workaholic real estate broker, living…on the moon.

That is not "positive-self talk," Julia, she reminded herself, echoing the words of her latest self-help book. Unfortunately, though, it was true, she thought.

They stood staring at each other for a long silent moment. Julia felt her eyes get watery and struggled not to cry.

"Well…thanks for stopping by. I'm glad we were able to talk," she said, trying for a friendly "no hard feelings" tone.

"Goodbye, Julia," Sam replied.

Then he stepped forward and cupped her face with his hands. He stared into her eyes a moment, and she couldn't even take a breath. He turned her face up toward his, then he kissed her. Softly at first, slowly and sensuously, as if he was sipping fine wine. Or tasting some rare delicacy he truly craved and never got enough of.

Julia slipped her arms under his leather jacket and wound them around his waist. The pressure of his kiss grew harder, hungrier. She heard herself softly moan in answer as she melted into his strong embrace.

The kiss deepened and she felt a deep flash of need, their attraction going from zero to 110 in mere seconds. Julia's head spun. Her hands roamed restlessly over his back, her body pressed even closer, his arousal unmistakable.

The couch.

They could move over to the couch very easily….

Suddenly, he pulled away. His expression was unreadable. His eyes bright.

She felt stunned and suddenly chilled, his warmth removed so abruptly.

"It's getting late…. I'd better get on the road."

She followed him to the doorway of her office, then remained there, watching him walk through the outer office to the front door.

"Right… So long. Have a safe drive," she called after him.

He waved briefly as he let himself out.

But didn't answer.

## Chapter Six

What had she done?

She'd ruined everything!

Julia paced around her office, shaking her head, pulling at her hair. She covered her face with her hands and screamed out loud. And was thankful that no one was around to hear her.

"I am such a blooming idiot!" she shouted at the ceiling. "I am a—a total, unmitigated…ass! What did I do?"

She caught sight of her reflection in the window. She looked like a madwoman and felt even crazier. Her tightly wound hair hung down her back, half-undone. Her eye makeup was smudged in big black circles and one hoop earring had somehow been lost in action during Sam's toe-curling kiss.

She dropped into her desk chair, not knowing if more screams and shouting, or just some good old-fashioned crying, was about to take her over.

Was she more upset about Sam? Or about her mother and

Lester? It was hard to decide as her thoughts bounced from one disaster to the other.

"I've ruined everything. She'll never forgive me," Julia sniffed, thinking about Lucy.

It didn't seem to matter now if Lester had balked at the prenup because his intentions were less than honorable. Julia hadn't dared raise that possibility with Sam. She had expected some tension between the older couple. But not a flat-out broken engagement.

She picked up the phone and quickly dialed her mother. Lucy picked up on the first ring. "Hi, Mom. It's me, Julia," she said quickly.

"Julia…? You sound funny. Coming down with a cold or something?"

Julia blew her nose. "Yes…I think so. I must have caught a bug."

The "buttinski" bug, most likely.

Lucy sighed. "I think you work too hard. I tell you that all the time, but you never listen to me."

"Yes, maybe."

Julia could tell Lucy was angry. Usually, at the first sign of the slightest sniffle, her mother reeled off a list of cold care instructions, then ran to her fridge, pulled out containers of orange juice and homemade chicken soup and drove right over to Julia's house.

"So…are you calling to check on my progress with Lester? I did as you told me, Julia. I asked him to sign a prenuptial agreement. He was very insulted and hurt, as I had predicted he would be," she pointed out. "He said if I don't trust him, or believe that he really loves me, our marriage doesn't stand a chance. He says he waited twenty-five years to meet me. His soul mate. But how can soul mates stand a chance without faith and trust?"

Lucy's words had dissolved into a halting, sobbing blur.

Julia felt like crying, too. That Lester, you had to hand it to him. He was probably the most poetic appliance repairman in the county. Maybe even the entire state.

Julia bit her lip and took a breath.

"I'm sorry, Mom…. I never thought Lester would take it quite that badly."

Unless he really was only interested in your money, Julia added silently. Perhaps this was a good thing after all. Perhaps the prenup had flushed out a silver-haired and silver-tongued gigolo. But she wouldn't dare say that now. It would only make Lucy angrier.

And she did feel sorry for her mother. Very sorry.

Her mother didn't answer. Julia heard her sobbing and sniffing. "He dropped me, Julia. He dropped me like—like a hot potato…."

Julia sighed. Her mother was in shock. One minute she was Lester's hot tomato and the next, a different vegetable all together.

"Can I take you out to dinner or something?" Julia offered, trying to speak over the sniffling sounds. "Or over to the outlet mall? I think you should have some company tonight, Mom. Some distraction."

"No, thank you. I'll be fine," her mother said briskly.

Wow, was she mad. She didn't even want to go shopping.

Lucy didn't get angry easily but when she did, watch out.

"I'm going next door to Eleanor's for a card party. Though I'm sure I won't be able to concentrate. I hope I'm partnered with Eleanor. She never gets annoyed."

Lucy was and had always been a terrible bridge player, even when her spirits were high. She really only played for the socializing and her friends were patient enough to include her.

"As long as you have something to do. It will be good for you to see your friends," Julia added.

Lucy sighed. "I can't tell them about Lester. I'll be mortified. I'll just wait a few days. Until my emotions settle down a bit."

Julia hadn't thought about that. Lucy's relationship with Lester was quite an achievement in her circle and the envy of her single friends. It was humiliating to her to be abruptly dumped when she was still busy spreading the word of their engagement.

"Who knows, in a few days, Lester might change his mind and you'll get back together again."

"Oh...I don't think so," Lucy said in a very serious tone. "You should have seen him. He was crushed. Just...heartbroken. He's a very proud man. Very emotional and sensitive. Not like most of the other men I've known..."

Like father, like son, Julia thought with a sigh.

"Give him time, Mom. Give yourself some time, too. This relationship has been a whirlwind. So much happening so fast. Try not to worry. Things will work out for the best," she promised.

Had she missed any comforting platitudes? Julia thought she ought to stop off at a card store and study up on helpful phrases for the coming days.

If Lester was the man Lucy thought he was, he'd come back, at least to talk things out. If he wasn't...well, Lucy was well rid of him and Julia knew she'd soon be distracted by someone new.

Next time she stopped over at her mother's house, Julia promised herself to secretly toss a fork down the garbage disposal.

"I've got to run," Lucy said abruptly. "I look like a wreck. I don't want them asking a lot of questions, either. I'm so ashen. I look like a ghost. I need more makeup. My false eyelashes or something..."

False eyelashes? This was serious.

Lucy's voice trembled but she didn't start crying again.

"Okay, Mom. I'll let you go. Call me if you'd like some company this week, or just want to talk. Okay?"

"Okay." Lucy's voice had a pouting tone. She said goodbye and hung up.

Breaking up with Lester had been a blow. It would take Lucy a few days to regain her equilibrium. Julia knew Lucy wouldn't let her off the hook anytime soon. She was going to pay for this miscalculation for a long time.

Even Sam—whom she'd only known for what...three days?—had cut her more slack and been more understanding of her intentions.

Had it only been three days? It certainly felt as if she'd known him much longer. They had spent some real quality time together, though. That counted for a lot....

And how easily would she get over Sam? Their time together had been more like taking an exhilarating ride in a hot air balloon...then jumping out. Julia wasn't sure she'd hit the ground yet.

She straightened up her desk and filled a briefcase full of mind-numbing paperwork, preparing to fill the empty hours before she could sleep tonight.

She'd just put her coat on when the phone rang. She thought it might be her mother again, changing her mind about her card party and wanting a daughterly shoulder to cry on after all. She picked it up and said hello.

"Sorry it took me so long to call back, Jules. I tried you at home and didn't get an answer, so I thought I'd try you here again. Working late on some big deal?"

Julia had rarely felt so happy to hear her best friend Rachel's voice. "There's a big deal going on all right. But it has nothing to do with real estate...."

She quickly filled Rachel in on Sam's visit, Lester dropping her mother like a hot potato and her call with Lucy.

"Poor Julia. All of that happened since I spoke to you this afternoon?"

"Would I make this stuff up?"

"I have some news that will cheer you up. Carey is here. She can only stay one night. She really wants to see you."

Carey Mooreland had been the first tenant to rent the cottage behind Rachel's store. She'd arrived in Blue Lake the past October with her baby daughter, Lindsay. She'd seen an ad for a part-time bookkeeper at the realty office and stopped by. But the job had already been filled. Julia heard her story, how her husband had died in a construction accident a few months before Lindsay had even been born and how she needed a job, even part-time.

Julia's heart had gone out to her and she immediately thought of Rachel's store and the cottage behind the store that Rachel needed to rent.

Rachel was just starting to need some sales help, especially with the holidays approaching. Lucy sometimes worked there as a salesperson, but her schedule was so scattered, Rachel needed someone more reliable. Rachel also needed help with her accounts, with sales taking off.

Carey was perfect for the job and the ideal tenant. She loved the cottage and the day-care room Rachel had set up in the store, where Lindsay ended up being Charlie's first best friend.

It had all worked out perfectly for a few months. Carey was easily one the sweetest people Julia had ever met and the three women had grown to be very close friends. But Rachel and Julia had never known Carey's real story, how she was being stalked by a man back in Cleveland, Quinn McCauley, and how she had witnessed illegal dealings in Quinn's business accounts tied to a bogus mortgage scheme that defrauded banks. Her knowledge had put her in danger, and had sent her on the run.

It was Christmas Eve when Carey had disappeared. Rachel and Jack had invited their closest family and friends to their new home, for a Christmas Eve celebration…and a small but lovely wedding ceremony.

Carey had left a note saying she'd been called away on a family emergency and would call them very soon. But they didn't hear from her for months. Meanwhile she'd had her own amazing adventure, stuck in Maine during a snowstorm. Hiding from the man who pursued her, Carey had found love with law officer Ben Bradshaw and a whole new life. The only tie remaining to her unhappy past was a need to give testimony for Quinn's trial.

"She's going to stop here on her way to Cleveland. Of course she's nervous. She said it would help a lot if she could see us on the way down. Are you free?"

"I'd love to see Carey. And you know my calendar is clear."

Rachel ignored her dry tone. "Great. I thought I'd make dinner for us here. That way we can relax and just hang out. Jack said he'll keep Charlie out of our hair."

"I never mind having Charlie with us. Even in my hair," Julia said honestly. The little guy did like to yank her locks once in a while. But she never minded. "He's a sweetheart."

It was men over two years old who seemed difficult to deal with.

"Don't worry. I'm sure you'll get to see him. And you don't have to bring any present, Aunt Julia," Rachel reminded her.

"Hmm…we'll see." She never met her little pal without a special surprise. She already had her eyes on an adorable stuffed dog with the saddest eyes. She'd spotted it in the window of the toy store in town. Was the shop still open? she wondered.

"Carey left Lindsay with her in-laws in Maine. But her husband, Ben, is here. He's going to hang out with Jack and watch football. Wait until you meet him."

The way Carey described him, he sounded like a superhero and movie star wrapped into one. But of course, she was madly in love.

"I'll be over in a little while, I just want to close up here," Julia promised.

Dinner at Rachel's house with Carey was an unexpected and remarkable surprise. A soft landing at the end of a long, rocky Monday. It was a bit hard for her right now to be with friends who were both happily married with children. But they were her closest pals. She didn't feel jealous, just wished it would happen for her, too.

When Julia arrived at Rachel's house, Rachel opened the front door and stood aside. Carey greeted Julia with a huge hug and all Julia's gloom seemed to disappear. It was so good to see her friend again after all these months. Carey's smile had always been pure sunshine. How had Julia forgotten that?

"Carey…I can't believe it's really you."

"It's me all right. You guys aren't getting rid of me that easily."

Carey turned to the man standing right behind her. "Julia, this is my husband, Ben."

He stepped forward and shook her hand. "I've heard a lot about you, Julia."

"All good I hope?"

"The best," he promised. He smiled and she was faintly reminded of Sam. Both men were tall, dark and...extremely handsome. Ben was more conservative and serious-looking than Sam. Even without his uniform on, she would have guessed he was a law officer.

She smiled but inwardly sighed. Would she go through the rest of her life comparing every handsome, dark-haired man to Sam? Comparing every man, period, to him?

Jack came forward and kissed her cheek. He was holding Charlie in his arms and Julia nuzzled her favorite boy in the crook of his neck, making him laugh.

"Look who's here, pal. Is it Santa? No...pretty close. Aunt Julia," Jack teased her.

"Since you brought it up, Jack, I do happen to have a little surprise for him." Julia produced a bright blue gift bag filled with tissue and a furry dog paw sticking out.

"What do you think is in there, Charlie?" Julia asked, handing him the bag. "I hope it's friendly."

Charlie eagerly pulled at the tissue and pulled out his new toy. "Doggie. Mine." His happy declaration made the adults laugh.

He hugged the new dog to his chest and Julia knew she'd made a good choice.

"Say 'thanks,' Charlie," Jack reminded him.

"Tanks," Charlie repeated. Then he leaned over and kissed Julia on the cheek.

"Oh, my. Thank you," she said in return. The surprise kiss was better than a bouquet of long-stemmed roses, she thought.

"He loves his Aunt Julia," Rachel told Carey. "She's going to spoil him rotten."

"Excuse me?" Julia defended herself with a laugh. "I'll have to wait in line. With his dad buying him all that fancy sports equipment? He just teethes on the baseball gloves."

"A boy needs to start early with sports. Especially these days." Jack glanced at Ben, looking for male support on this question.

"Which reminds me, isn't it game time?" Rachel smiled and gave her a husband a look.

Jack and Ben each checked their watches. "Right. See you later, ladies," Jack said. Then he led Ben back to the spacious family room and huge flat-screen TV. Julia gathered that they were both die-hard fans of the New England Patriots and had a lot to talk about.

Carey sighed and rolled her eyes. "Male bonding. Isn't it a beautiful thing?"

Rachel laughed. "As long as the New England Patriots exist, they'll never lack for conversation."

Julia smiled, wondering if Sam was a football fan. He didn't seem the type. But you never know. There were so many things about him that she didn't know. And would never find out now.

The three friends went into the kitchen and enjoyed some wine and conversation, catching up on the last few months, while Rachel finished making dinner.

Rachel was not a fancy cook, but a very good one. She'd made one of her specialties, pot roast and noodles. "I know we're probably all on diets, as usual. But it's such a chilly night. I felt like cooking something hearty."

Julia didn't protest. She was thankful for some comfort food. She was also thankful that Carey had so much to tell them about her new life up in Maine. Ben's family owned a hotel and Carey worked there now, part-time, helping his mother, Thea, and sister, who ran it.

While they ate, Rachel answered Carey's questions about what was happening at the shop and filled her in on all the latest gossip in town.

Julia knew it was her turn to jump in. Lucy's engagement was certainly a hot item. Though, as far as she knew, Rachel was one of the few who knew that the wedding plans had already been called off.

"My mother got engaged again," Julia told Carey. "To her appliance repairman."

Carey looked surprised and amused, as Julia had expected. "Is he a nice guy? Do you like him?"

"I've only met him once. A few days ago. The night they announced their plans... I was surprised, to say the least. I mean, I didn't even know she was dating anyone."

"Oh. Well, that's rough. When do they plan to get married?"

Julia sighed. "The whole thing is off right now. And...I'm to blame."

"Julia, come on. You can't blame yourself. Not entirely," Rachel stated. "Julia was concerned about her mother and persuaded Lucy to ask for a prenuptial agreement. But when she did, her fiancé got insulted and called the whole thing off."

"Oh...gee...what a mess." Carey cast Julia a sympathetic glance. "Now I guess your mother is mad at you?"

"You've got that right. Though at least we're on speaking terms." Julia sighed. The worst part about it seemed to be Sam—and their "slam-bam, thank you, Ma'am" encounter, which had left her reeling.

Rachel seemed to read her thoughts. "There's more to the story," she told Carey. "Lester has this gorgeous son, Sam. He's a chef. He came to Julia's house and made dinner...and, well... one thing led to another."

Carey's eyes lit up with interest. "Wow. Interesting. A chef, huh? Do you like him?"

Julia took a long moment before answering. She glanced at each of her friends, then nodded her head. "I do...but I made a mess of that, too." She sighed. "I've been trying to meet a guy I really like for years. Then I just lose it over this one. I have no idea why, but…he's totally wrong for me. Even if you try to ignore this huge mess between our parents, which is really impossible to ignore. And now he's left town and I'll never see him anyway…."

Her friends listened patiently while she babbled, each reaching over to pat a hand. Finally, Julia's explanation of Sam dissolved into hiccupping sobs.

Rachel ran to the sink and brought her a glass of water. "I think you have to hold your nose while you drink it."

"I heard you drink it with your head upside down," Carey said. "Then you breathe into a paper bag?"

Julia stared at both of them and started to laugh through her tears. "There is no cure for hiccups. It's a scientific fact." She paused, and was overtaken by another thought. "You just have to wait for them to pass on their own…."

"Like feeling horrible over a man," Carey offered.

"Same principle," Julia agreed. Then she hiccupped again.

Rachel's look was loving and sympathetic. "I'm sorry it didn't work out. But I think it's a good sign that you were just swept off your feet, Jules. A very good sign."

"You do?" she asked, pressing her hand over her mouth. "Why is that?"

Rachel shrugged. "Because when it comes to men, I think you think too much. I like the idea that this one made you lose your mind. I think that's a very positive sign. Don't you, Carey?"

"Definitely," Carey agreed. "It's enough trouble having a relationship. If you aren't madly in love, why bother?"

Rachel laughed. "Good point."

Julia smiled but didn't reply. For one thing, she was afraid that all she could manage was another hiccup. For another, she didn't agree. She didn't like the feeling of losing all control, feeling her reasoning and reserve in a complete meltdown. It was…scary.

But apparently, her friends believed otherwise. They'd both fallen wildly in love and married the man of their dreams.

Who was she to argue with success?

Rachel made coffee and brought out dessert—a homemade apple pie and vanilla ice cream. They heard a roar from the family room. "Either something awfully good, or something really bad just happened," Carey interpreted.

"Should I call them in for coffee?" Rachel asked.

"I think they're glued to the screen right now," Carey said knowingly. "They wouldn't notice pie and ice cream if you smeared it over yourself and walked through the room naked."

"I tried that last week when dinner was getting cold. Of course, it was only stew and mashed potatoes. Maybe dessert would work better?"

Carey and Julia laughed at Rachel's flat comeback.

It did feel good to be with her friends tonight, to tell all about Sam and have a good cry. And a good laugh.

Julia heard her cell phone. She pulled it out of her sweater pocket and checked the number. It didn't look familiar but she flipped the phone open and answered, expecting a client or attorney on the other end. "Julia Martinelli," she said.

"Julia? It's Eleanor Weeks. Your mother asked me to call you," Lucy's neighbor began. "Your mother isn't well. She's been taken to the hospital."

Julia felt frozen, shocked. She felt the blood drain from her head to her toes. "What happened? Did she fall?"

"She had some chest pains and trouble breathing. We called 911 right away…."

Julia's heart dropped. "Did she have a heart attack?"

"I'm not sure, dear. She may have. They took her to Lake Grove Hospital. I'm there with her now. She's conscious and they've started tests."

"Tell her I'm on my way. I'll be right there," Julia promised. "Thank you, Eleanor. Thanks for your help."

"No problem, dear. I'll wait with her. Don't worry."

Julia closed the phone and stared at her friends. "My mother is in the hospital. It sounds like she's had a heart attack."

Her friends stared back at her with shocked faces. Julia could barely believe it herself when she said the words aloud.

Poor Lucy. She'd been so upset about Lester…it had literally broken her heart.

This was all her fault. Why couldn't she just have let her mother be romantic and idealistic and trusting? Why did she have to walk around, smashing everyone's rose-colored glasses? As if that was her only mission in life.

If anything happened to Lucy now, Julia knew she would never forgive herself….

## Chapter Seven

Julia jumped up from the table, looking around for her purse and coat. "I've got to go. Sorry…"

"Jules. Wait…You can't go alone. You're too upset. I'll drive you over," Rachel said.

"I'm coming, too." Carey stood up and grabbed her coat from a hook by the back door.

Julia thought to refuse their offer, but honestly didn't want to be alone. She wasn't sure what she would find at the hospital. She didn't even let herself imagine.

She always prided herself on her independence, but this was one time she was willing to put her pride aside and simply appreciate the support of her friends.

A few minutes later, the three women set off in Rachel's SUV for Lake Grove Hospital. The drive was less than an hour from Blue Lake. The three friends had gone from talking nonstop to near silence as they sped along the dark highway. Julia was so worried, she could hardly speak.

Rachel dropped Julia at the emergency room entrance and drove off to park. Julia found the admitting desk and asked about her mother.

"Lucy Martinelli. She came in by ambulance a little while ago, with chest pains…."

While the nurse behind the desk worked on a keyboard, Eleanor Weeks appeared at Julia's side. Eleanor was a tall, slim woman with short gray hair, bright blue eyes and a gentle, calm manner.

The Weeks family had lived next door for as long as Julia could remember. Eleanor had always been the type of person you'd call first in an emergency. When Julia was a teenager she secretly wished Eleanor was her mother. Their neighbor seemed so sensible and levelheaded. More like herself.

But at that moment, the wish seemed shallow and immature. Lucy had her faults, but Julia wouldn't change her for the world. She felt awful for not appreciating her mother more and being a more understanding daughter.

"You got here fast," Eleanor greeted her and kissed her on the cheek.

"My friend drove me. How's my mom? Have you seen her yet?"

"Just briefly. I told her you were on your way. She's still having tests. The doctor said he'll come out when they're done."

Julia nodded. She squeezed Eleanor's hand. "Thanks for staying with her. Thanks for everything," she added.

"That's all right, dear. Don't worry. I think she's going to be okay."

"I hope so," Julia said. Rachel and Carey came through the entrance together and walked over to meet her. She introduced them both to Eleanor.

"I see you have some company," Eleanor remarked with a smile. "I guess I'll go then. Keep in touch, Julia. Let me know how she's doing."

"Yes, I will. Thank you."

Once Eleanor left, they found seats on the vinyl couches in the waiting area. It was fairly empty, Julia noticed. A TV hung from the ceiling in the far corner and most of the other people waiting were gathered close to it.

Rachel and Carey sat down on either side of her. "I guess I just have to wait now. You guys don't have to stay, honestly. I'll figure out some way to get home later."

"Of course we're staying," Rachel said. Carey nodded.

They sat quietly for a moment.

"This is all my fault," Julia said. "I shouldn't have forced her to confront Lester. She really didn't want to…I talked her into it."

"Jules, you can't blame yourself for Lucy getting sick. This might have happened if she was perfectly happy tonight, picking out wedding invitations. Or taking a bubble bath. I know it's hard to believe, but you're not being logical."

"She's right, Julia," Carey said. "No one knows why these things happen. It can happen to anyone. Anytime."

Julia nodded. She knew they were both just trying to help her get through this, to be good friends and say the right things. But she did blame herself, no matter what anyone said.

If only her mother pulled through this crisis, she'd never meddle in Lucy's life again. Even for her mother's own good.

A man in green surgical scrubs walked toward them. He was tall with gray hair and wire-rimmed glasses. Julia noticed a stethoscope slung around his neck and a folder in his hand. She assumed he was a doctor and hoped he was Lucy's.

"Julia Martinelli?" he asked, taking in the three women with a searching glance.

"I'm Julia." Julia stood up and walked to meet him.

"Dr. Newman. I'm the cardiologist treating your mother." He extended his hand and Julia shook it, feeling nervous about what he might report.

"How is she? Did she have a heart attack?"

"She's resting comfortably right now. The blood work and

electrocardiogram indicate that she did have an episode. We've given her some medication to stabilize her heart."

An episode. That was a nice way of saying heart attack. Julia felt her stomach drop.

"Can I see her?"

"You can visit for a little while. She was just moved from the emergency area to a room in intensive care. She never lost consciousness. That was fortunate." The doctor opened the folder and scanned a sheet of notes. "We need to do more tests to check her arteries and valve function. She may have a blockage. Or more than one, actually."

"That doesn't sound good. What will you do then?"

"We'd probably recommend surgery. But let's just take it one step at a time."

"Yes, let's," Julia agreed.

Surgery? That was serious. Julia suddenly thought she might cry.

"She'll have the rest of the tests done tomorrow. Unfortunately there are no technicians here tonight. But it's not an emergency," the doctor assured her. "She'll be taken down first thing in the morning. I suggest you come back around noon. The tests will take a few hours."

"Okay," Julia said. She'd expected to come back early in the morning but that left her time to tie up loose ends in the office. If her mother did have an operation, she'd definitely be off work for a few days.

"I'll stop by to see your mom sometime late tomorrow when I've gotten the test results back. I have an office in the hospital if you need to get in touch sooner."

"Thank you." Julia thought she should have found the doctor's cool, analytical manner a comfort. But for some reason, she didn't.

She found out her mother's room number from the admitting desk, then told her friends she was going up to visit. Again, they insisted on staying and wouldn't leave without her, no matter what she said.

Julia took the elevator to the third floor, the cardiac care unit. Her mother was in an intensive care area. The nurses on duty seemed very strict and said she could visit for only a few minutes.

Julia was led to her mother's bed but wasn't prepared to see Lucy hooked up to so many machines. Lucy looked small and fragile in the big hospital bed, her head rested on the pillow, her eyes closed. Her face was bare of makeup and her hair had lost its usual "fresh from the beauty parlor" style. She looked very fragile and sick. Julia felt shocked again, thinking how close she'd come to losing her.

"Mom…I'm here. How are you feeling?"

Lucy's eyes sprang open and she turned her head. "Julia. Oh, my. That was a scare. One minute, I was playing bridge, trying to figure out how to bid, which you know, I'm awful at…and the next…" She swallowed. "Luckily, Eleanor knew exactly what to do. I'm not sure what would have happened if…"

Julia interrupted her, not wanting to hear the worst-case scenario. "I spoke to your doctor. He thinks you had a heart attack. You're going to have more tests tomorrow to see if any arteries are clogged."

"Yes, he explained that to me." She sighed. "I really don't want an operation."

"Well, it might not come to that," Julia said, though she had a feeling it would. "Let's just take it step by step," she added, repeating the doctor's advice.

"I've been lying here thinking. Of a lot of things, actually." Lucy had lived a full life and Julia could only imagine. "You're a good daughter, Julia. I love you so. I know I can be very difficult at times. Very childish and impulsive…still, I'm very lucky to have such a sensible, caring child like you looking after me."

"Mom…" Julia squeezed her hand. "I'm so sorry…. This is all my fault. If I didn't start meddling with you and Lester, this would have never happened."

"Oh, hush. That's not true. It's not you. Or Lester, for that matter. It's my own nasty cholesterol. I haven't had it checked for over a year and the doctor said it's through the roof. He nearly fainted when I admitted I still ate…BLTs."

"You do make a mean BLT, Mom." Julia had to smile.

Lucy sighed. "Your father's favorite. Of course, I'm sure his new wife uses some sort of tofu bacon and fake mayonnaise."

Julia felt certain she was right on that score. "Do you want me to call Dad and tell him you're sick?"

After all these years, Lucy and Julia's father had a cordial relationship. Julia was sure he'd want to know if Lucy was seriously ill.

Lucy sighed. "Oh…I suppose you can. But don't make a big deal about it. Call him tomorrow, after we know what's what."

"Okay," Julia agreed. "What about…Lester? I'm sure he'd want to know, too."

Lucy's expression grew harder. Julia could tell she was still mad at him. "Don't you dare call him. After the way he treated me…what's done is done." She glanced at Julia. "I'm no genius at picking men, dear. I'm finally ready to admit it."

"Oh, Mom…"

"No, let me finish. I think the jury is still out on Lester. Maybe he did have good intentions and was just too proud to deal with a prenup. Or maybe it was what you suspected all along," Lucy added. "I'm not proud of being married so many times. Jumping onto the first log that comes floating down the river every time."

The image made Julia want to laugh. Mostly, because it seemed so true.

Lucy glanced up at her. "I wish I was more independent. Like you. But I'm too insecure. I get so lonely," she admitted. "I'm not able to stand on my own two feet and take care of myself. Like you are, dear."

"Oh, Mom. That's okay. It's just the way you are. I think it's… good. Really," Julia insisted, patting her mother's hand. "It's not so great being Miss Independence all the time. It's good to fall in love and open your heart to someone else. You have to be brave to do that, too. Sometimes I think I've met plenty of men I could have been happy with. I get scared and run away."

"Oh, honey. You may have met plenty of guys. But you haven't met the right one. You're just so special. You need someone who's extraordinary, like you are. And extraordinary men don't grow on trees."

Julia nodded. One man who could fit that description came to mind. And she'd already decided their relationship would never work. What were the chances of meeting another like him anytime soon?

Julia sighed. It felt good to exchange confidences with her mother this way. When was the last time they'd had an honest, open talk like this? It had taken a crisis to bring it on, but it was at least a small silver lining.

She still couldn't admit her feelings for Sam to her mother. But she could confide something she had never dared mention before.

"I'm not getting any younger, Mom. I really want…a baby," she confessed. "And I'm not sure I can wait for Mr. Right, if you get my drift."

Julia watched her mother's expression. Lucy watched daytime TV. Julia could tell she got her meaning.

"You mean you want to be a single mother by choice? Is that what they call it now?"

Julia nodded.

"Who would be the father…if I may ask?"

"I'd use a sperm bank. It's a lot…easier that way."

"Find a father at a sperm bank? Like your friend Rachel?"

"I've been thinking of it," she confessed.

Lucy looked surprised. She didn't say anything for a moment and Julia wondered what she was thinking.

"If that's what you really want to do, Julia. I'll help you any way I can. If you make me a grandmother, I'll be so busy, I might even need to give up my hobby."

"You mean shopping?" Julia teased her.

"No, silly. Getting married."

"Oh, Mom…" Julia shook her head, feeling as if she was laughing and crying at the same time.

A nurse stuck her head in the door. "I'm sorry, Ms. Martinelli. Your mother needs to rest now. I've let you have some extra time, but you need to go."

Julia nodded. "Okay. I understand."

She turned to Lucy, bent over the bed and kissed her cheek. "Good night, Mom. See you tomorrow. Don't worry. Everything is going to be okay," she assured her.

"All right, dear. If you say so," Lucy said agreeably.

Julia could see that her mother was truly tired and Lucy closed her eyes before Julia had even reached the door.

Julia returned to the hospital the next day at noon, as the doctor had suggested. She went to the intensive care unit, but learned her mother had been moved to a private room.

A good sign, she thought hopefully.

When she arrived at the room, she heard voices inside— Lucy's voice and the deeper voice of a man. Was it the doctor already? They didn't expect to see him until later this afternoon. A faster appearance had Julia worried.

But when she came through the doorway, she saw Lester. He sat on a chair close to Lucy's bed with his head leaning down on her shoulder. Lucy's head was tilted toward his and she gently stroked his cheek. He appeared to have been crying and Lucy's eyes looked wet and red-rimmed. She must have been crying, too.

Julia jumped back into the hallway, feeling embarrassed to interrupt their private moment. They obviously had not noticed her peeking in.

Despite her good manners and ethics, and even better judgment, she couldn't help lingering a moment, listening to what they were saying.

Julia wondered how Lester had heard the news that Lucy was in the hospital. But they did know people in common. Eleanor Weeks, for one. And Lucy's friends didn't even know that Lucy and Lester had broken up, so maybe they'd called him just to see how he was dealing with it.

"It's okay, dear. Please don't cry anymore. Lester," she heard Lucy say. "It's my cholesterol. The doctor said it's through the roof."

The same explanation she'd given to me, Julia noticed. Her mother's cholesterol count was taking the rap for everyone.

"But I shouldn't have flipped my lid over the prenup idea. Couples have to talk things out when they disagree. That's the first thing you learn about a good marriage. Looks like it's been so long for me, I forgot rule number one."

Julia was impressed. Not only was Lester right about talking things out, but he could also admit when he'd been wrong. That was a quality Julia found rare in people. Especially men.

"I was a stubborn old fool, Lucy," he said flatly. "You were only trying to protect yourself. It's true that we haven't known each other very long and a woman alone has to be careful."

"Well…it was Julia's idea," she heard her mother remind him. "But she meant well. Honestly."

"Of course she did," Lester agreed. "She was just looking out for you. I love you truly, Lucy," he stated flatly. "I'll sign anything if you'll marry me. I'll give up the farm idea. It didn't take me too long to realize I'd rather have you than a herd of goats any day."

Lucy laughed. "Well…thanks. I think."

He laughed, too. Julia was glad they had both stopped crying, though she did feel a little misty-eyed herself.

"The important thing is that we love each other and share the rest of our lives together. Will you marry me? Please?"

"Oh, Lester…get up off the floor. You'll get marks on those nice pants," Lucy scolded him. "Of course I'll marry you. I love you. I always will," she promised.

Now Julia did feel her eyes fill with tears. To hear two people confess such emotion. Knowing for her mother, "always" may not be very long at all...

It just got her all choked up.

Which usually didn't happen. Not even in a mushy, romantic movie.

She didn't hear any more talking and guessed they must have been embracing to seal the deal.

Then she heard Lester say, "Wait a minute. I almost forgot..."

Then Lucy gasped, loudly sucking in a long breath.

Julia nearly rushed in, thinking her mother felt more chest pains. But she quickly realized it was a gasp of pure delight.

"What a perfectly beautiful ring! Lester, it's gorgeous! I always wanted a sapphire...."

"None of your other husbands gave you one?" He sounded pleased by the news.

"Nope. I had a diamond, of course, from Tom. A ruby from Earl. A little cultured pearl from George—he was such a cheapskate." Julia could just tell from the sound of her voice she was making a face. "Then another diamond again from Ralph. I skipped sapphires all together. The one gem I always wanted."

"Then it was meant to be. Just like you and me, honey." Lester laughed, sounding pleased. "We saved the best for last, Lucy," he said sweetly.

"Yes, we did, dear," she agreed.

"Try it on, let's see how it fits."

"Perfect. Look how it sparkles. Oh, I wish I could get a manicure.... I doubt that's available here."

Julia sighed. It was so good to hear her mother happy again. That alone had to be a boost to her health. To her immune system and all those nasty chemicals that built up in her body when she was stressed and unhappy.

*Okay, maybe I've had my doubts about Lester. But he does seem to be the perfect medicine,* she thought.

Julia surmised it was a good time to make her entrance. She strode into the room, loudly clearing her throat. She glanced at Lester, doing her best to feign a wide-eyed look of surprise.

"Lester, gee…the nurse didn't mention Mom had any visitors."

"Hello, Julia. I heard your mother was sick and rushed right over." He stood up from his seat and walked over to her.

Julia felt a bit awkward facing him and he seemed to feel the same. But he smiled, then leaned over and gave her a quick hug.

"I'm sorry you had such a shock last night. If I'd known, I would have been here in a flash."

"Oh…thanks. I was all right. My friends drove me here and stayed until I knew Mom was all right."

He nodded, then quickly dabbed his eyes with a hanky. It seemed that just talking about Lucy's close call stirred up his emotions.

"My girl's a fighter," he said, glancing back at Lucy. "She's a champ. She's going to come through this with flying colors. We're going to get married. Right, Lucy?"

Lucy nodded. "We've talked things over, Julia. We've worked everything out. Look…Lester, gave me the most beautiful ring."

A sapphire, Julia nearly said aloud. But she held her tongue.

"Let me see," she said curiously, walking to her mother's bed. "Oh, my…what a beautiful stone."

"I've never had a sapphire before. It's always been my favorite. Lester just guessed."

Lester beamed with pride. "Nothing but the best for Lucy."

The ring was impressive, a large square-cut stone flanked by diamonds. Perhaps Lester had a larger nest egg than she'd imagined, Julia realized. If the ring was any indication, he really didn't need Lucy's money.

Her mother smiled, holding out her hand and admiring it again. And looking much better than she had the night before, with more color in her cheeks.

"You look much better than last night, Mom," Julia said.

"I have to give Lester credit for that." Lucy smiled at him.

"How did the test go?"

Lucy shrugged. "Oh, those people working the machines are nice enough. But they never tell you anything. Not allowed, I suppose. We have to wait for the doctor."

"Whatever it is, we'll face it together." Lester took Lucy's hand. "It's going to be okay."

Lester's simple words gave her mother comfort, Julia could see, and it was a relief to have someone there, helping deal with the crisis. Julia was always alone in these situations.

Yet, somehow Julia realized she still felt alone. Lester was entirely focused on Lucy, as it should be, of course. She didn't want to be mean-spirited or self-centered at a time like this, but at that very moment, she did secretly wish there was someone interested in comforting her.

A sharp knock on the doorframe drew everyone's attention.

"I have to ask your guests to leave now, Mrs. Martinelli." A nurse walked in carrying a tray with little paper cups of pills. She smiled briefly at Lucy. "It's time to check your vitals and take your meds."

"It's like the army in here," Lucy whispered. "They're always marching in, telling you what to do."

"Just do as they say, dear. So you can get better and we can get hitched." Lester dropped a kiss on her forehead.

The nurse stepped up to the other side of the bed and wrapped a blood pressure cuff around Lucy's arm.

"Nurse, did you see my ring? I've just gotten engaged. To this nice man right here."

"Congratulations," the nurse nodded, glancing at Lester then at Lucy's hand. "Please keep your arm down."

Lucy put her arm down, still gazing at her ring. "It's a sapphire," she added.

The nurse didn't reply, jotting down Lucy's pressure on the chart. She looked up at Lester and Julia, as if noticing they were still there. "She needs some rest now."

"Yes, of course. See you later, Mom." Julia kissed her mother's cheek. "I'll bring you some magazines."

"Thanks, dear…can you find this month's *Cosmo?* I didn't get a chance to read it yet."

Julia struggled not to smile. Still studying up on the Seven Sexy Secrets Sure to Drive Him Wild! Julia wondered what they were this month. Lucy sure didn't seem that sick.

Banished from Lucy's room, Julia and Lester walked down to the elevator together. Julia didn't know what to say. She wondered if Lester disliked her now, seeing her as a troublemaker. He would have every right.

She glanced at him. He seemed pensive, focused on Lucy, she guessed. She punched the elevator button to go down. "Guess I'll get some coffee."

He looked up at her and nodded. "Not much else to do around here. Mind if I join you?"

"Not at all."

They got out at the first floor and followed the signs to the hospital cafeteria. It was almost empty and they took their paper cups to a small table by a window. It was a dreary, late-winter day, nickel-gray clouds hanging low in the sky.

Julia tried hard not to let the weather get her spirits down. But it was hard.

"Feels like snow again," Lester said as he sipped his coffee. "When you get older, winter seems longer. When I retire, I'd like to get a place somewhere hot and sunny for a few months out of the year, skip all this New England winter. I've paid my dues, believe me."

"Sounds good to me," Julia said agreeably. "But my mother hates Florida. Don't even mention it to her."

"Good tip. Thanks," he nodded, looking grateful. He looked suddenly serious again. "I'm sorry we got off on the wrong foot, Julia. I should have known better at my age. Guess I'm just a crazy old fool in love, rushing things. At our age, you don't want to wait. It's worse than being a teenager."

"Yes, I can see that," Julia said drily.

"It's important to me that you and I get along. Understand each other. We already have a lot in common. We both love your mom," he added.

Julia nodded. She believed him now. He did seem to care sincerely for Lucy. It wasn't just an artful act with a hidden agenda.

"I know you have your doubts about me. If I were in your shoes, I might feel the same. All I ask is that you give me a chance, just a little time to prove myself. I've always believed actions speak louder than words. I think you'll see that I'm a good guy. My only wish now is to marry your mother and make her happy and take care of her."

Julia nodded. She didn't know what to say. "I believe you, Lester. My mother doesn't have the best track record with men, so maybe you can understand why I'd be so concerned."

"I'll admit, when Lucy first told me how many times she'd walked up the aisle, it did throw me. But once I heard her story and got my mind around it, I saw all those other relationships as a long winding path she had to take to meet me." He smiled. "She wouldn't be the woman she is now without all those experiences, adding layers and patina, like a masterpiece hanging in an art gallery somewhere. She's my Mona Lisa," he added with a grin.

"That's very wise, Lester. That's a very thoughtful way of looking at it." Julia was honestly surprised at his response. So thoughtful and accepting.

How did a man get to be so wise gazing into broken appliances all his life? Lester truly had a poetic soul.

Lester smiled. "I've always thought that the right person comes along when you're ready to meet them. I've been a widower for twenty-five years. I had my share of romances, my own winding path to follow. But I knew I'd never reached the end and met the right one. 'Til Lucy came along." He shrugged. "That's just the way it is."

Julia wondered how long it would take for her to meet the right one. Twenty years? She hoped not. She sighed.

Lester reached over and patted her hand. He obviously thought she was worrying about her mother.

"Don't worry, Julia. I'm here to help you now. We're practically family."

"Thank you, Lester. I appreciate that," she said honestly. "I'm anxious to hear what the doctor will say."

"I am, too," he said quietly.

She took a last sip of her coffee and put the cup aside. "I'd better go find that magazine she wanted. Maybe some nail polish. I'll see you back up at the room."

"Sure, dear. See you later."

Julia left Lester and headed for the hospital gift shop.

She gazed at the row of magazines. The mind-numbingly bright covers covered with celebrity faces and outrageous headlines put her in a trance. She picked up three for her mother, *Cosmo* and two celebrity tell-alls. Then one for herself, a home magazine. Not that she had much time for cooking and crafts and decorating projects. But leafing through the pages helped her fall asleep at night.

Perhaps it would calm her while she waited today to hear Lucy's prognosis.

Upstairs, she found Lucy asleep, the room darkened. She sat out in the waiting room for visitors a few doors down the hall. She called her office on her cell phone and checked in with Marion. It was a quiet day, thank goodness, with no emergencies.

"How's your mother doing?"

"She's good, much better than last night," Julia reported. "We're waiting now to hear what the doctor says."

"Oh. Well, good luck."

"Thanks. Just one more thing," Julia said before she hung up. "You're sure there were no other calls?"

"That was it. Just the Watsons, Anita and that lawyer about the DiMarco closing."

"Okay. I just wanted to double-check. Thanks. I'll call you tomorrow morning."'

Of course Sam hadn't called. Why would he? Even if Lester had told him Lucy was in the hospital, that didn't mean he'd call *me,* Julia reasoned. Not the way we'd left it. Not after I blew him off so...so unconditionally.

He wasn't heartless. She was sure he felt sorry to hear that her mother was ill. But he'd get all his updates through Lester. He certainly didn't need to call her directly.

So...why had she even nurtured a tiny, slim hope that he would?

Because you're feeling scared and lonely right now, Julia. Buck up. No one is going to gallop in on a white charger and save you. Not even...Lester. You have to face this on your own. Just like you always have.

Julia called Rachel at the store, but the machine picked up. She guessed Rachel was busy with customers or Charlie and couldn't answer. She left a quick message and opened her magazine.

She hadn't gotten too far—she'd barely found the table of contents among all the advertisements—when she spotted Dr. Newman coming down the hallway. The doctor forced a smile and nodded at her. Julia had a feeling the news about her mother was not good.

A few minutes later, she stood in her mother's room along with the doctor and Lester, who had come upstairs just in time for the consultation. He stood by Lucy's bedside and held her hand. Lucy looked frightened and Julia's heart went out to her.

"The test you had today confirmed what I'd suspected. You have three arteries that are blocked and we need to open them up right away, Lucy...."

The doctor continued with a more detailed explanation of the problem and the type of surgery he thought would be most effective. He explained that Lucy needed bypass surgery, as opposed to angioplasty, which was much less invasive.

"Your situation requires more extensive surgery. We have to open up your chest wall and reattach the clogged arteries to healthy ones. But it's also a common procedure and very successful. You have no other health problems, like diabetes, for instance, that might complicate your recovery."

Julia sat down on the edge of the bed. She had a feeling this was coming, but still felt stunned to hear the doctor say her mother needed major surgery. Life-threatening surgery, she knew, though he was trying to put the best face on it.

"How long will take for her to recover, Doctor?" Lester asked.

"If everything goes well, she'll be out of the hospital in just a few days. Then it will be a few weeks before she's back to her regular routine."

"That doesn't sound too bad, Mom," Julia said, giving her a mother an encouraging smile.

Lucy nodded, but her chin was trembling. Lester not only held her hand now, but also patted her back reassuringly with his other hand.

"The good news is that a terrific cardiac surgeon happens to be in the hospital right now, performing another surgery. I've already spoken to him about you and we can schedule your procedure for a few hours from now. In your case, this isn't exactly a choice. But you do need to agree on this course of treatment. I strongly suggest you don't delay and go forward with the surgery tonight."

Lucy nodded, her chin trembling. "I'm sorry, Doctor. Maybe I should have expected this news, but it's a lot to think about."

Lester looked worried. He stood by Lucy's side, patting her hand. Julia wondered what he was thinking, if he was going to encourage her mother to wait, or go forward. Julia didn't want her to wait, which she thought was ironic since she was clearly the least impulsive person out of the three of them.

"If my mother doesn't have the surgery tonight, when could she have it?"

"A few days from now. I'm not even sure I can keep her in the hospital that long. You know how tough the insurance companies are these days. She might have to go home and wait, which is dangerous since she's at risk of another heart attack."

"Oh…I've lasted this long. I didn't even know I was sick," Lucy said.

Julia bit her lip. She knew what the doctor had said was true. Right now her mother was hooked up to all kinds of monitors that went off at the nurses' station if she so much as sneezed.

She looked over at Lucy. "You need to have the surgery tonight, Mom. It's too dangerous to wait."

Lester glanced at her. "I think Julia is right, dear. It's better to get it over with. I don't think I could stand a few days of waiting and then bringing you back here."

"I have to agree with your daughter and…" The doctor didn't know what to call Lester. Julia realized they hadn't even been introduced.

"Lester is my mother's fiancé," she said quickly. "They're going to be married very soon. As soon as Mom recovers."

Lester met Julia's gaze with a small smile. He seemed to appreciate the way she'd acknowledged him. She felt the tension and ill feelings between them were almost erased.

"Your family is right," the doctor continued. "I think you should listen to their advice."

Lucy looked down at her lap and sighed. Julia could tell she was struggling with the decision. But when she finally looked up at everyone, she seemed resigned.

"Okay, I'll do it." She shrugged. "Might as well just get it over with. The faster I'm out of here, the sooner I'll be on my honeymoon."

Lester laughed. "That's my girl. We'll go wherever you say. You just name it."

Julia breathed a sigh of relief.

Then she felt anxious all over again, considering the long night of worrying that lay ahead.

Once Lucy agreed to the operation, everything seem to go on fast forward, like hitting a button on the remote control, Julia thought. There were documents to sign and more tests needed before the operation.

The surgeon came in to introduce himself and explain the procedure and what to expect in more detail. Finally, orderlies arrived to wheel her mother downstairs and prep her for surgery. That would take some time, as well, but it was now the last they'd see of Lucy for several hours, until the ordeal was over.

Maybe the last she'd ever see of her mother, Julia realized. She felt tears fill her eyes and struggled not to show her mother she felt any fear. It was important that her mother entered into this battle with positive thoughts and expected total success.

She stood at the side of her mother's bed and gripped her hand, then kissed her cheek. Her mother looked scared but forced a smile.

"Remember how scared I was the first day of kindergarten?" Julia asked her Mom.

Lucy nodded. "Oh, dear. Yes, I do. You were terrified, holding on to my leg like you'd never let go."

"Remember what you told me? I do," Julia said quietly. "You said, 'Don't be afraid. I love you and it's like a magic cloak, wrapped around you all the time, protecting you from anything bad. So you never have to worry.'"

Lucy nodded and smiled, her eyes shining. "Yes, I did tell you that. It seemed to work, didn't it?"

"It did. And now I'm going to tell you the same thing." She glanced over her shoulder. "And Lester feels the same way, too, so you have two magic cloaks covering you. Imagine that."

Lucy smiled. "I will imagine that. Right before they put me to sleep, that's what I'll be picturing, dear."

"I know you'll be fine, Mom. Don't worry…I love you," she added.

"I love you, Julia. You're my pride and joy. I've told you that since you were a baby and it's still true. Don't worry, honey. You're not getting rid of me so fast," she added with a jaunty laugh. "Is she, Lester?"

"Absolutely not," Lester agreed. Then it was Lester's turn to wish Lucy good luck. They hugged and kissed and whispered to each other.

Julia looked away, giving them a private moment.

"Sorry, folks. Time to go," the attendant finally said.

Lucy's resolve seemed suddenly shaky. She couldn't let go of Lester's hand.

"Can he go with me down to the elevator?" she asked an attendant.

"Sure. That would be okay," the orderly said.

"Do you want to come, Julia?" Lester asked kindly.

Julia shook her head. "No…that's okay. She needs you now, Lester. I understand."

Then Lucy was wheeled out of the room with Lester walking alongside. She glanced at Julia and blew her a kiss.

"See you later, Mom," Julia said, summoning up her most positive tone.

Suddenly the room was empty. The bed where her mother had been lying in disarray, the machines all unhooked and silent.

Julia wasn't sure what time it was. The sun had set long ago and there was only one low light on in the room near the bed. Julia had struggled hard to hide her worry and anxiety from her mother, keeping a tight wrap on her feelings. But now she felt herself suddenly melt down and lose all control.

She stood with her back to the door and burst into tears. Could she actually lose her mother tonight? The idea was unthinkable—but possible, she knew, no matter how the doctors tried to sidestep the issue, calling it a "risk factor."

Julia felt a cold wave of fear wash over her, making her tremble. She covered her face with her hands and felt her body shake with sobs, crying as if she'd never stop.

She wasn't sure how long she'd been sitting there when a gentle touch on her shoulders caught her attention. She turned, expecting to see Lester. Or maybe a nurse.

It was Sam, his dark eyes filled with emotion.

She stepped back, not knowing what to say. Was she just imagining him here?

"Sam…what are you doing here?" she asked quietly.

"My father called this afternoon. He told me that he and Lucy had made up. But Lucy had a heart problem and might need an operation."

Julia nodded. It was hard to say the words out loud.

"She needs surgery to open up her arteries. They just took her down. It will be a few hours before we know anything."

He didn't answer. Just stepped toward her and rested his hands on her shoulders. His dark gaze swept over her face, studying her. Something in his expression melted her last shred of reserve.

She threw herself into his open arms, burying her face in his shoulder. She felt him hug her tight, nearly lifting her off her feet.

"Sam…I'm so afraid," she whispered. "But I'm so happy that you came…."

"So am I."

He found her lips with his own and kissed her. She felt as if she'd never let him go.

## Chapter Eight

Lester, Julia and Sam waited together during Lucy's operation in a small private room reserved for patients' families. The doctors had explained the procedure would take several hours. Julia felt so nervous, she wasn't sure she would last. But it did help to have Sam there. Throughout this crisis with her mother, he'd never been far from her thoughts. And now, here he was. As if her longing to see him had conjured him.

Lester was happy to see his son, too, but not nearly as surprised as Julia at his arrival.

"I told him he didn't have to come. I'd be fine," Lester explained. "But that's Sam. If you're in trouble, he's there. You don't have to ask twice."

Sam looked mildly embarrassed by his father's praise, Julia noticed, color rising in his lean cheeks. "Anybody hungry?" he asked, changing the subject.

Despite the fact that Sam had left the city in a rush, he'd still managed to pack two shopping bags filled with food for them to share—gourmet sandwiches, salads, fruit and miniature pastries. He opened the bags and served them as if they were in a fancy restaurant, complete with linen napkins and silverware.

"I figured we'd all feel miserable enough without having to eat in some hospital cafeteria," he explained.

"Good thinking, Sam." Lester bit down on his sandwich. "I don't know why, but these situations always make me so hungry. Must be the stress."

"Yes, I think it is," Julia agreed.

She glanced at Sam. She hadn't felt any appetite at all before his arrival. But now, she did feel hungry and was grateful for his thoughtfulness.

"This looks delicious," she said, meeting his glance for a moment. "Thank you for going to all this trouble."

"It wasn't any trouble." He sat down next to her, across from his father. "It was the least I could do for you."

She glanced at him but didn't answer. After the way she'd spoken to him before he'd left town, she knew he didn't have to do anything for her. But he was obviously not the type who held a grudge. Or else he wouldn't have come at all, she realized.

Nobody spoke very much, even after they were done eating. They were all too worried about Lucy, Julia realized.

After the way she and Sam had parted on Monday, she had expected to feel very awkward if she ever saw him again. Now, here he was and it somehow seemed easy and expected, as if they'd never parted on angry terms just two days ago. As if they'd never parted at all.

She did feel a strong, indescribable connection with him. Something that went beyond mere physical attraction and sexual chemistry. Something that just…clicked.

Sam was here and she was happy about it. That was all she knew for now. She didn't want to analyze or worry about any of that right now. She was too focused on her mother, wishing and praying every second that the operation would turn out okay.

There was a TV in the room and Lester and Sam watched a football game. After a while, Lester got up from his chair.

"I'm too riled up," he said honestly. "I've got to take a walk. Get some air."

"Want me to go with you, Dad?" Sam asked.

Lester waved at him and put on his coat. "You stay here and keep Julia company. In case they come in with any news. She shouldn't be alone."

In case it was bad news, Julia knew he meant. She didn't even want to think about that possibility.

Sam watched him go. Then he shut off the TV and looked up at Julia. "If anything happens to Lucy, he'll be devastated."

"Yes. I know." She took a breath and looked up at him. "I'm sorry I ever doubted your father. I can see now how much he loves Lucy. I'm ashamed now for the way I suspected him. That was wrong…I guess I really just don't do well with surprises," she finally confessed. "That engagement announcement just pushed my buttons."

Sam smiled slightly. "I surprised you today. You seemed to deal with it okay."

Julia tilted her head back and gazed up at him.

"Seeing you again pushed other buttons," she admitted. She sighed and looked away. "We didn't part on a high note, did we?"

"No…we didn't. But I came anyway. For my dad, of course. But for you, too, Julia—" He paused and met her gaze. "Maybe this isn't a good time to get into this. I know how worried you are about your mother."

"Yes, I'm worried. I'm on pins and needles, waiting for someone to come in here and tell us what's going on." She turned to him. "Maybe that's why I have even less patience to wait to hear what you want to say. Now that you've brought it up. Go ahead." She tossed her hands in the air. "You can't just say something like that and expect me not to be at least curious."

"Curious?" He nearly laughed. "Well, I guess that's a start."

He paused for a moment, his handsome face wearing a serious expression again. "I had some time to think things through the past few days. I decided I shouldn't have rushed you into bed."

Julia sat up straight, her eyes wide. "Rushed me? I wasn't exactly an unwilling partner. As I recall, I practically ripped your clothes off...."

She blushed to admit it. But it was true. She didn't like being portrayed as some frail flower who'd been overpowered. If anything had overpowered her that night, it had been her own wild longing for him.

Sam smiled, a flash of light in his eyes signaling that he, too, had fond memories of their night together.

"Believe me, I'm not saying that at all. But emotionally, I'd guess it wasn't your usual speed, Julia. Or you wouldn't have run off that way the morning after. But it wasn't my usual speed, either," he added. "Not with anyone that matters."

She mattered to him?

Was that what he was trying say? Julia felt a stirring of hope in her heart, like the sound of tiny silver bell.

"I think you made all these assumptions about me, Julia. That I'm some kind of...operator or something. Just to protect yourself. The way you did about Lester. Just to protect your mother." He sighed. "I guess I'm trying to say...I've been thinking about you a lot the last few days. At first, I wished I wasn't. But I couldn't seem to get you out of my head. So I came here to be with you because I care about you. And I wish you would give our relationship another try. From square one."

Julia met his gaze and couldn't look away.

She swallowed hard, not knowing what to say. Her heart did a pirouette of sheer joy when it suddenly sunk in—that despite her misery at the way she'd screwed things up with him, he'd still been thinking about her. He still wanted to give their fragile, fledgling, misbegotten romance another try.

Then her rational side muscled in, insisting she stick to the original plan. Sam Baxter was not the end of her winding path. Just a tempting pit stop. She had no more time to waste on interesting side trips. Not if she wanted to meet a man who would settle down and give her a baby. She was on a tight schedule now to meet that goal.

But how could she actually stand here and tell him, with a straight face, that they weren't right for each other? It would never work out. And besides, he lived too far away. All of the well thought out "goodbye and good luck" lines she'd delivered the other day?

How could she dare repeat all that now, after the way she'd flung herself into his arms the minute he looked at her?

Julia sighed. She'd given away far too much of her hand in this game. She was a terrible card player, just like her mother.

She had best fold and admit she was beat.

"I think we've already given it another chance, Sam. The minute you found me crying in that hospital room. I think we've probably made it to square two at least by now," she said quietly.

He looked pleased by her answer, and the glow in his dark eyes made her heart race.

"I thought so, too…but I needed to hear you say it."

He stepped closer and rested his hands on her waist, then softly kissed her lips. Julia closed her eyes, losing herself completely in the sensation of his warm mouth moving over hers. Finally, she pulled away, tucked her head under his chin and pressed her cheek to his chest. He stroked her hair with his hand.

"If feels so good just to hold you like this…I missed you," he admitted.

Julia silently agreed.

The door opened and Lester came in. He glanced at them, then looked away, seeming embarrassed. "Oh…sorry to interrupt. I should have knocked or something…."

"It's all right, Dad," Sam said simply.

Julia took a breath and stepped away from Sam. She wasn't

sure what Lester knew about her and Sam, or what he thought…if he did know the whole story. But Lester definitely had a poetic soul and seemed to be in favor of romance wherever it struck.

A knock sounded on the door, then a nurse walked in. "Ms. Martinelli?" She looked at Julia with a reassuring smile. "Your mother is doing very well. The procedure is going well and so far, it's successful."

Julia felt her entire body sag with relief. "Thank you. That's wonderful news. Thank you very much," she repeated.

Lester slapped Sam on the back. "I knew she would make it. That little lady is tougher than she looks, believe me."

"It's good news," Sam agreed. "All good."

There was nothing to do but wait for the final word that Lucy was out of surgery and in the recovery area. Lester paced around a few minutes, jingling the change in his pockets.

"Mind if I turn on the TV again?" he asked. Both Julia and Sam shook their heads.

"Fine with me, Lester. Go right ahead," she said.

He picked up the remote and found an old movie—*Casablanca.*

"I love this film," Lester said, settling back in a plastic arm chair. "They don't make them like this anymore."

"It is a good one, Dad," Sam agreed. He glanced at Julia. "It's a beautiful romance. Did you know they filmed two endings? One where Bogart and Bergman stayed together and one where they part. Not even the actors knew which one would be used in the final version."

"No, I didn't know that," Julia answered. Was he trying to tell her something? She was too tired and stressed to puzzle over hidden messages.

She took a seat on the couch and stared at the set. Sam sat next to her. Before Julia realized it, her head fell back and her eyes closed. The last thing she remembered hearing was Bogart's gravelly voice saying, "Here's looking at you, kid…."

She suddenly woke up with a start. Someone was softly calling her name. She felt Sam's arm around her and realized she'd fallen asleep with her head cushioned on his strong, wide shoulder. She wasn't even sure at first where she was, then remembered.

"How's my mother, any word?" she asked quickly, turning in Sam's embrace.

"We're about to hear something more. The nurse is coming back."

Julia looked over at the doorway just as the nurse from the surgery floor walked in. She was smiling, which seemed a good sign.

"Mrs. Martinelli came through the operation just fine. Her pressure is stable and she didn't lose much blood. The surgeon is closing the incision and she'll be moved to the recovery area shortly. She's still under anesthesia and won't be able to speak. But you can see her if you'd like to just take a peek."

Julia rose quickly. "I do want to see her."

"Me, too," Lester said.

They all left the waiting room and followed the nurse down to another floor. Then waited a few minutes more outside large swinging doors that had a sign that read No Admittance.

A large clock on the wall showed the time. It was nearly two in the morning. Julia felt as if she could fall asleep right on her feet. Only the thought of seeing her mother and making sure she was all right kept her alert.

Finally, they were admitted one by one to the postsurgical recovery area. Julia went in first.

Her mother lay on the gurney, her hair still covered by a paper cap, a blanket pulled to her chin. Julia could see the edge of white bandages on her chest. She wondered how long it would take her mother to heal.

Lucy's eyes were closed and Julia took her hand. She looked very small and frail lying there and Julia felt a chill, realizing she could have lost her. Just when it seemed they were growing closer.

Julia had heard that patients under anesthesia or in a coma

could hear people talking to them, even though they didn't respond. So she leaned over and tried it. It made her feel better, too.

"You're going to be all right, Mom. You came through the operation fine and you're going to have a long, happy life with Lester. And…you're definitely going to enjoy your grandchildren," she whispered in Lucy's ear.

That was one dark thought that had crossed her mind tonight. She might finally have a baby and her mother wouldn't be around to help her or to enjoy being a grandma.

That seemed to be a false alarm. Julia was thankful.

She stroked Lucy's cheek. "I love you, Mom. I really do."

Finally, she stood up and walked back to Lester and Sam. Sam handed her a tissue without saying anything. She smiled and dabbed her eyes.

"How does she look?" he asked.

"Better than I expected," she admitted.

Lester's focus was on the closed doors of the recovery ward.

"I'm going back to check on her," he said. "Then I think I'll wait around until she wakes up. You two ought to go on home. Come back after you had a few hours' rest."

"The nurse said it could be a while, Dad. You'll end up sleeping here."

"I know. I already asked. The nurse said I could sleep in her room in a chair. I won't sleep a wink if I go home now. I'll be worried about her all night."

Julia was again amazed at his dedication. She'd had the same thought about staying until Lucy woke up but was surprised when Lester said it first.

"I can stay, Lester. I was planning on it."

"You're all worn-out, dear. You can hardly keep your eyes open. You let me. I want to. Besides, I've been drinking that awful cafeteria coffee all night. I'll be up whether I stay or not." He looked at Sam. "Take Julia home now, Sam. I think she's too tired to drive by herself."

"Yes, I will, Dad."

"So…you've decided for me?" Julia asked, once Lester had left them. She was not entirely pleased to be managed by two men. "You won't even let me drive my own car?"

"You've been through a lot today. It hasn't even all hit you yet," Sam said gently. "Can't I take care of you a little, Julia? I came all this way to do that," he reminded her.

She met his dark gaze and found herself persuaded.

A short time later, they were in his car, a black SUV, and headed back to her house. The road was empty, a long black ribbon winding through the mountains and the dark night.

Julia felt exhausted but struggled to keep her eyes open. Sam looked tired, too, she noticed. He had driven from Boston to Blue Lake today and had to be spent. He stared straight ahead at the road.

"It was good of your father to stay at the hospital tonight. He really is devoted to Lucy," she said.

He glanced at her. "He loves her with all his heart. When he called this afternoon to tell me she was in the hospital, he could barely get the words out." He glanced at her. "Do you still have doubts about his intentions?"

Julia shook her head, feeling embarrassed. "No…I don't. Not after tonight." She looked over at Sam. "Lester and I had a talk this afternoon. I apologized to him for the way I acted. He was very understanding."

"Good. I'm glad to hear that. One less thing for you to worry about. Funny how a crisis like this puts things in perspective."

That was true, Julia thought. And walls of reserve tumbled down and people started being honest with each other about their true feelings. Like herself and Sam.

They soon reached her house and pulled into the driveway. Sam shut the car and turned to her. "Here we are," he said.

"Thanks again for driving me home. I could have driven myself…but it has been a long day."

"At least the ending is better than the start," he added.

Did he mean the positive outcome of her mother's surgery? Or just the fact that they were ending the day together? Maybe both, she thought.

The way he was looking at her made her think that perhaps the day wasn't entirely over yet. She couldn't pull her gaze away from his, the warm light in his dark eyes filling her with heat. And longing for his nearness.

He moved closer, cupping her face with his broad hand, the pad of his thumb smoothing over her cheek. Her eyes closed, and she savored his touch. Then she felt his lips meet hers and his body close, one arm slipping around her waist, then moving up to cup her breast.

She sighed against his mouth, leaning herself into his caress. She wound her arms around his shoulders and pulled him closer. She felt as if everything was happening in slow motion…kissing him, touching him, unzipping his leather jacket and slipping her hands underneath his sweater to touch his chest.

Tired from the long day, she felt totally relaxed, her inhibitions dissolved. She didn't have the energy or the will to deny her desire. Her senses tingled, her body felt awake and aroused.

Finally, Sam lifted his head and stared into her eyes. "We're fogging up the windows now. Wow, I haven't done that since I was a teenager."

Julia nearly laughed. "Yes, it's getting pretty steamy in here. We'd better go inside before some snoopy neighbor comes out to investigate."

He stared down at her, then stroked some loose strands of hair off her cheek with his hand.

"You're sure you want me to come in with you? I'm not going to be mad if you say you don't. Though certain parts of me will definitely be…disappointed." His tone was light and wry. But the question marked a serious moment.

The moment of truth, Julia realized. The one she'd been expecting ever since he'd found her today in the hospital.

If she didn't want this man in her life, if she really thought they were entirely wrong for each other and there was no future in it, this was the moment to speak up.

Julia was too tired to think. Too tired to fret about consequences or the right thing to do. Perhaps inviting him in wasn't wise in the long run. But she couldn't worry about the long run now. Any other choice than lying in his warm embrace tonight seemed unthinkable.

All she knew was how she felt right then and there, lost in Sam's arms. All she knew was that she wanted him close to her. She couldn't bear to be parted from his warmth, his touch, the passionate kisses that stirred her soul.

"Come inside with me," she said quietly.

She was almost afraid to look at him, but finally couldn't resist.

In his eyes, she read his wordless reaction. It was as if a curtain had dropped, revealing an ocean of desire.


Julia woke the next morning with one of Sam's arms snaring her bare hips and his head next to hers on the same pillow, his slow, deep breaths stirring her hair.

She had no idea what time it was. She'd heard Lester's voice on the answering machine, leaving a message. He said it was about six o'clock and he was sure she wasn't up but wanted her to know her mother had come out of the anesthesia and was doing fine.

Julia meant to get up, but the news had eased her worries and she realized that so far, she'd only been in bed about three hours. And all of that time, she certainly had not spent sleeping.

She turned her head slightly to face Sam. The phone had not woken him and he was still far off in dreamland, his features a picture of peaceful repose.

He did have such a beautiful, darkly handsome face, the heavy shadow of beard on his cheeks and chin making him doubly irresistible. A man just didn't have a right to look that good at this hour of the morning.

She knew that given very little encouragement, she could

easily make love to him again. Just as if he'd heard her secret thoughts, his eyes opened slowly. He smiled at her and she felt his grip on her waist tighten.

"So, you're still here. What a pleasant surprise. A little different from last time," he said.

She didn't answer. She didn't want to admit that she was totally content lying beside him and in no rush to leave the bed. She rolled over on her side, brushing her long, smooth leg along his hair-roughed calf.

"Yes…here I am. Happy now?" she asked with a small smile.

He moved closer, his arm slipping around her waist and his leg moving between her thighs. "I am happy. Can't you tell?" He spoke quietly, his warm breath tickling her ear.

She could feel his body, hard and ready to make love again, and she felt herself ready, too, her nipples tingling and taut as his big hand moved up to cover her breast and his lips moved slowly down the curve of her neck in a slow, sensuous assault.

"I'll tell you what would really make me happy. To show you what you were missing the other day when you ran out on me, Julia. I mean, unless you're in a rush again this morning? Any pressing appointments?"

Julia moaned as his mouth covered the tip of her sensitive breast. Her hands stroked his broad, muscle-ridged back and then gripped his slim hips as she moved under him. He fit himself between her thighs and finally slipped inside of her.

She stared up at him, her hands framing his face. "I am in no rush," she somehow managed to say.

Then she closed her eyes and gave herself over to a wave of heat that washed through her body like a riptide.

Their joining was sweet and slow. Julia felt herself slowly rocked on an ocean of heat, each thrust pushing her to a higher and higher peak. Her entire body felt electrified, pulsating with white-hot pleasure. She didn't know how long she could stand it, the tantalizing climax dangling just out of her reach.

Finally, when it seemed as if she couldn't bear it another moment, Sam brought her to the brink. With one final thrust she felt her body arch and explode into a million tiny sparks of fiery light. She trembled in his arms, surrendering herself completely to the vibrant sensations.

Then she felt Sam reach his own peak, moving inside of her as he called out her name, then collapsed in her arms. She wrapped her arms around him and nestled her face in the crook of his neck, savoring the warm, solid weight of his body on top of her.

The next time she woke up bright stripes of sunlight showed under the edge of the bedroom shades. She knew it had to be late in the morning. The space in the bed beside her was empty and she heard the shower running.

She slipped out of bed and pulled on a robe, then went downstairs to the kitchen where she started a pot of coffee.

It was a few minutes past ten. Julia couldn't recall the last time she'd slept so late, but imagined that with Sam's late hours in the restaurant business, he slept until that hour often and probably even later.

Another difference between them—she was an early bird and he was a late bird. Though last night, their differences didn't seem to matter much, she reminded herself.

She was pouring out a mug of coffee when Sam appeared. He wore jeans and a light blue tailored shirt. His hair was wet and his shirt hung open over his bare chest. He walked up behind her and kissed her neck. "Good morning."

"Morning." She handed him a mug of coffee.

"Did you call the hospital yet?" he asked, settling on a stool by the counter.

"No, not yet. But your father called at about six and said my mother had woken up and was doing well."

"That's good news."

It seemed the crisis was past and Julia wondered when Sam would head back to the city. Perhaps as early as today?

The thought made her sad. And grouchy. She blew on her coffee and took a sip.

"Everything okay?" he asked suddenly.

She looked up at him. Was she that transparent to him? She shook her head. "Sure…I'm fine. I'm just thinking about work. I'd better take a shower and call the office," she said quickly.

That's right, Julia. Whenever you need to hide your feelings, go into the workaholic mode.

"I'll make some breakfast," he offered. "How about some eggs?"

"Sounds great. Everything you need should be in the fridge."

When Julia came back downstairs a short time later, she felt composed, her feelings under control once again.

Sam had prepared a large omelet and toast. While she'd often made the same dish, it never looked as good. His omelet was perfectly formed with tiny appetizing flecks of herbs in the golden folds of egg, and cheese melted within.

He'd set two places for breakfast and was sitting at his, reading the newspaper.

He looked up when she walked in. "How's the office? Holding together without you?"

"Everything is fine. Between you and me, I think they do better when I'm not there to interfere," she admitted. "I called the hospital, too. I didn't speak to your dad, but a nurse said my mother is doing well. As well as could be expected," she added. "She said the doctor was stopping by to see her soon."

She hadn't liked the nurse's measured tone, her carefully worded report on Lucy's progress. But Julia figured that the nurse was not allowed to say too much. That was the doctor's turf.

"She can only see visitors for a few minutes, once every hour. I guess I'll stay there today and try to see her as much as I can."

Julia wondered what Sam's plans for the day were. But she didn't want to seem too clingy by asking outright. She'd certainly been clinging to him last night, in every way possible. She'd never acted that way with a man before. He had not seemed to mind and had, in fact, actively encouraged clinging of all kinds.

But she still hoped he didn't think she was the needy type. Men always claimed they wanted to help out in rough times and even take care of her, but Julia had found that once she showed a man her vulnerable side, it always sent them running.

Would Sam be the same?

"I guess I'll call my dad on his cell." He picked up his empty plate and carried it to the sink. "I wonder if he's still at the hospital. He might want a change of clothes or something."

Sam took out his cell phone, then called his father.

Julia heard them speaking briefly. She couldn't hear what they were saying, only the tone of Sam's voice.

But her senses grew alert when his tone suddenly changed from warm and relaxed to seriously concerned.

"All right, I'll tell her. Yes, Dad. Don't worry. We'll be right there."

Sam closed his phone and turned to face her with a solemn expression. Julia felt the blood drain from her face.

"What is it?" She rose from her seat and walked toward him. "Did something happen to my mother, Sam?"

He gripped her shoulders. "Your mom has taken a turn for the worse, Julia. She's having some complications from the surgery. The doctor isn't sure why. She may have an infection."

"Oh…I see." Julia nodded. It was bad news. But not the worst. That was some relief. "I'd better get over there…."

She looked around for her coat and found it slung over the living room chair. Sam found her purse on the floor by the front door and handed it to her.

Julia never just dropped her belongings like that when she got into the house. But she had shed her usual neat-freak behavior last night. Along with everything else.

She felt Sam's hand rest on her shoulder in a comforting gesture. He glanced down at her and brushed her hair off her shoulder with his hand.

"Don't worry. Let's see what her doctor says. It's probably a common reaction to the surgery."

Julia nodded. "I hope so."

Julie suspected it wasn't a common reaction at all and Sam probably knew the same. But he was just trying to make her feel better and she appreciated it.

She was suddenly very glad that he was with her and she didn't have to face this latest emergency alone.

## Chapter Nine

The next few days passed in a blur of watching, waiting and worrying.

Lucy had caught a postoperative infection. Her doctors had immediately begun treating her with antibiotics. But it was a very strong germ, they explained, and Julia's mother was very weak after the surgery.

Julia, Lester and Sam stayed by Lucy's side day and night. But Julia often wondered if her mother was even aware that they were with her as she slipped in out of consciousness, her fever rising and falling, but never quite disappearing altogether.

Every hour was a battle and Julia wished with all her heart that she could somehow fight it, too. But it was Lucy's alone to win or lose.

Lester was distraught, practically inconsolable. He'd gone from a loquacious, upbeat soul to a sad, silent figure, hovering over Lucy's bed. Sam was in the middle of it all, comforting both his father and Julia. Somehow, taking care of everyone.

Sam drove Julia back and forth to the hospital whenever he could pry her away from Lucy's side. He fed her, put her to bed and even kept her from drowning one night when she nearly fell asleep in the shower.

Julia had never felt so cared for, so watched over, so supported by anyone. Not even Lucy, who had always been a very loving mother, but was a bit flighty and self-involved at times.

Sam's care was different altogether, nurturing with a totally masculine touch. When he held Julia close at night in her bed, curling his body around hers, she felt as if she was protected from every possible harm. She felt him willing his energy into her, to keep her afloat in a stormy sea.

When she did allow herself to sleep, she was totally exhausted. Most of the time, making love was not even an option. Though she wanted to very badly. She just couldn't keep her eyes open long enough.

"Unless you don't mind if I'm unconscious?" she once asked him.

Sam laughed. "While I find you completely irresistible, I'm actually not that desperate. Yet. It is more fun for me if you're awake enough to enjoy it, too."

"I'm sorry," she said, nestling her cheek on his bare chest. "Maybe in the morning?"

By the time he'd told her not to worry and kissed her good-night, she was fast asleep.

Julia was in touch with Rachel all during her mother's hospital stay, sometimes talking to her friend a few times a day. It was difficult for Rachel to leave the store during the day and since Jack had gone away on business the day of Lucy's operation, it was hard for her to leave Charlie at night. She came by on the second day that Lucy was in the hospital and then again on the fifth day, at night. She mainly came to see Julia, since family members only were allowed to visit with Lucy.

When Julia went down to meet her, Rachel greeted her with

a huge hug. Julia pulled away, and she could see that her friend was misty-eyed. "Oh, Jules…I feel so bad for you. And for Lucy. How is she doing? Any improvement?"

"Her fever is still up and down. She recognized me and was able to say a few words." Julia had seen these flashes of improvement before, though, but they hadn't lasted long.

Rachel knew the same. "That's good news. Let's just hope she keeps improving. How are you holding up? Is Sam still staying with you?"

Rachel had heard a lot about Sam but had yet to meet him.

"Yes, he is," Julia said quietly. She wanted to add that he had to be the dearest, sexiest, most loving and patient and understanding man in the world.

But all she could manage to say was, "He's been…great. It's been a big help to me."

Rachel nodded, a knowing look in her eye. "Sounds like this has possibilities after all."

Julia felt her cheeks color. "Maybe," she admitted.

Rachel's gaze suddenly swept to the entrance and Julia saw her eyes widen. Julia turned and followed her glance. She saw Sam walking toward them. He met her gaze and smiled widely.

"Is that him?" Rachel whispered. Julia nodded. "Wow…and you said he cooks, too? How lucky can you get?"

Julia struggled not to laugh at her. "Shh…he'll hear you."

By the look in his eye when he reached their table, Julia knew Sam had already guessed they'd been talking about him. Julia quickly introduced them. Sam smiled at Rachel and shook her outstretched hand. Then he quickly turned his attention back to Julia without even bothering to sit down.

"I have some great news. Lucy's fever finally broke. She took a nap while you were down here and when she woke up, her temperature was normal. She's sitting up, alert and talking. She's asking for you," Sam added.

Julia felt so happy and relieved, she could hardly believe it.

She jumped out of her chair and flung her arms around Sam's neck. "I can't believe it…finally."

"Oh, Julia, that's great. I'm so happy," Rachel said.

Julia glanced at her friend and nodded. She realized she was crying, but happy tears this time.

"I'd better get upstairs. She must be wondering where I am." Julia headed for the exit, and Rachel and Sam followed.

When they reached the elevator, Rachel hugged her. "Call me later when you get a chance. Give Lucy my love."

"I will," Julia promised.

The elevator ride seemed so slow. Sam took her hand and Julia squeezed his fingers. He smiled at her, but didn't say anything.

When the doors opened, she raced out and ran straight to her mother's room. Lucy was indeed sitting up in bed, Lester sitting next to her.

"Mom…" Julia couldn't say anything more. She ran to Lucy's bed and hugged her as best as she could, considering all the tubes and monitor attachments.

"I'm so happy you feel better. You gave us such a scare."

"She scared me half to death," Lester said. "But I knew she'd come out of it."

Julia could see that he'd been crying, but, again, tears of joy this time.

Julia felt the same, but she wouldn't let herself cry so openly. Sam came up behind her and put his arm around her shoulder. Her first impulse was to hold back her emotions, not to let anyone see what she really felt. Then she relaxed into Sam's soothing touch, his hand drawing slow circles on her back. For once, she let go. She cried and laughed and hugged Lucy again.

"You always keep me on my toes, Mom. I have to say that for you."

Lucy smiled, not able to laugh yet. "You're getting better with surprises, dear. I really think so."

Dr. Newman knocked on the door and walked in the room

carrying Lucy's chart. He was very pleased with Lucy's progress and looked relieved, Julia thought.

"The new drug we tried is finally working. The infection is contained. I'm going to order some more blood tests to make sure, but I think we've made it through the worst of it now."

Julia breathed a long sigh of relief. She glanced at Sam and he smiled wordlessly at her. How would she have made it through these last few days without him? Well, she would have done it somehow. But she would have been a different person, cleaving to her independence like a badge of honor, meanwhile feeling so lonely and empty inside.

Julia and Lester stayed with Lucy as long as the nurses would allow. Sam stayed for a while, too, then excused himself when his partner in Boston called.

Julia realized she'd been so focused on her mother the past few days, she hadn't asked Sam a single question about his business, the restaurant start-up, and if it was hard for him to take such a long leave.

Finally, the nurse came in and told all of Lucy's visitors it was time to go. Even Lester didn't argue. He was too exhausted to stay. They all kissed Lucy good-night and Julia felt relieved to feel her mother's forehead so cool to the touch.

"See you tomorrow, Mom. Get some good rest."

"You have to concentrate now on recuperating, dear. I'm bringing the planner book tomorrow. We're going to get to work on the wedding," Lester announced.

"Yes, Lester," Lucy said brightly. "I'm ready."

Julia glanced at them. A little over a week ago, she'd practically flipped out at the same announcement. This time, her only reaction was a wide smile and a silent sending of her blessings. Funny how things change, she realized.

Down in the parking lot, Sam offered to take everyone out to dinner to celebrate. But Lester begged off. "You two go ahead.

I'm going straight home and hit the sack. I feel as if I could sleep for a week."

He did look tired but happy, Julia thought. He had been so loyal to her mother during the past few days, she felt embarrassed all over again for ever doubting his sincerity.

"So, what do you say, Julia? Want to go out and celebrate?" Sam asked.

Julia moved closer and tipped her head back to look up into his eyes. She rested her hands on his slim hips.

"Why don't we just go home and relax? I'll make you dinner for a change," she said.

Sam slipped his arms around her waist, picking up her signals. "Hmm…that's an offer I can't refuse. Though I'm thinking now that by the time I'm finished *relaxing* with you, we'll just send out for pizza…and eat in bed."

"Good point." Julia rose up on tiptoe and softly kissed his lips. "I feel intimidated by the idea of cooking for you anyway."

He held her close and laughed. "Sweetheart, you could serve me bread and water. I'd love every crumb."

Then he kissed her and Julia felt lost in their embrace. Lost, but somehow, happily found.

Her mother's crisis had been horribly frightening, one of the worst moments of her life. Yet, something good had come out of it, too, Julia thought. She'd finally figured out that she could neglect her office for days on end and the building would not collapse into a heap on Main Street. In fact, business was better than ever.

She also learned that it was okay to fall apart sometimes, to let someone else prop you up and keep you going. To let yourself be vulnerable and trust someone that much. The way she now trusted Sam.

It took a certain kind of courage to be that honest and unin-hibited. She'd never been able to find it before. But with Sam, she somehow could. Did that mean she'd fallen in love with him?

She gazed over at him, seated next to her as they drove back to her house. She wasn't sure. Or maybe she just wasn't willing to admit that much yet, even to herself. But the feelings she had for him were strong and even frightening to her.

She knew they were opposites in so many ways and there were a million practical reasons why it would be hard for their relationship to last. She didn't even know if he wanted a child or had any interest at all in being a father. Or being committed to a woman in any real way.

But she couldn't imagine her life without him now. He hadn't said a word about the future. She secretly hoped that even at a great distance, even without any commitment, they could somehow continue what they'd started.

When they reached her house, it was Julia's turn to take charge and take care of all Sam's needs. Even though she was tired from the past few days, she felt a sudden surge of energy and even exhilaration. She was happy about her mother's outcome for sure. But it was more than that. All her loving feelings and gratitude for the way Sam had taken care of her, all her pent-up wild desire for the dark, handsome man who had stood by her so staunchly came spilling out in a practical way.

She opened the front door with her key and then took him by the hand. "Let's go upstairs," she said softly, leading the way.

"Don't you want to check your messages? There might be some from work," he teased her. He knew her routine by now.

Julia shook her head. "I have some important business to take care of right here. Up in the bedroom."

Sam didn't need to be asked twice. He had his arms around her and had begun undressing her, before they'd even reached the bedroom door. Julia eagerly began undressing him, too, between deep, hungry kisses. She pulled off his shirt and slipped his jeans down his long lean legs.

They fell together on the bed, entwined in each other's arms, clothes trailing on the floor behind them.

Sam stroked her body with his hands, his hot mouth fastened

on her taut nipple. Julia moaned with pleasure, her body coming instantly alive at his touch.

Then she took a deep breath and pushed him to his back, so that she was on top. "Not so fast, pal. I told you it was my turn tonight."

Sam's expression was amused and delighted. "Right. Sorry... I got carried away."

Then he couldn't manage another word as Julia's moist mouth roamed over his hard chest, her tongue swirling across a flat male nipple, her hands caressing his taut stomach and thighs. Her mouth wandered lower, teasing and taunting him.

He tried to touch her, but she pushed his hands away. She knew her turn would come. Right now she wanted to give him complete pleasure and let him be the total focus of her attention.

Sam stretched back with a sigh and let go completely. His body became her playground.

She felt him hard and hot in her hand. She stroked and pleased him. Then she moved her mouth over him, pleasuring him in his most sensitive places. She heard him moan with ecstasy and he writhed in exquisite pleasure.

Finally, he couldn't hold back any longer. His body clenched and exploded as he reached his peak. She felt his hands in her hair, and she pressed her cheek to his stomach, just laying there for a moment until he caught his breath.

"When you put your mind to something...watch out."

"I told you I was going to take care of you tonight." She lifted her head and swung her long hair over her shoulder.

"Yes, you did. But I didn't realize that meant I was going to feel like I died and went to heaven."

Julia felt herself blush. She knew that when it came to Sam, it was different than with other men. Not that she wasn't a giving and attentive partner. But her feelings for Sam made her so much less inhibited and simply inspired her.

"Time to order the pizza?" she asked.

He shook his head. "No way. Now it's my turn. That's only fair, don't you think?"

He already had his mouth on her breast, twirling her nipple with the tip of her tongue, his other hand slipping between her legs, his fingertips caressing her feminine core as if stroking silk.

Julia took in a sharp breath. She couldn't answer his question. She couldn't manage another intelligible word.

The next morning Julia found herself alone in bed. She pulled on her robe and went down to the kitchen, following the scent of freshly brewed coffee. Sam was in the kitchen, showered and dressed, looking very handsome with a fresh shave and his hair combed back wet.

He was talking on his cell phone, making notes on a pad. He smiled briefly at her, his eyes lighting up in that special way that always made her pulse race.

She filled a mug with coffee and sat at that kitchen island, waiting for him to finish his call. She felt her stomach rumble. She was probably just hungry, she thought. They'd never managed to call out for that pizza and she hadn't eaten any dinner at all.

Finally, Sam snapped his phone shut and walked to her. He put his arms around the back of her chair and pressed his face into her neck, kissing the sensitive spot under her ear.

"You smell good," she said. "I like that aftershave."

"You smell even better," he murmured. "I wish I could drag you back to bed."

Julia sighed and smiled. He cupped her breast with his hand over her thin silk robe. Then he lightly kissed her lips and slowly took his hand away.

He sat down next to her and sighed. "I have to leave today. That was my partner. We've found a place we like and he's been negotiating a lease. He says if we don't sign, we'll lose out."

"Oh…sure. I understand." Julia nodded, trying her best to be calm and even supportive. "Well, if you like the spot and the price is right, you'd better grab it," she said.

She grabbed her coffee and took a long sip, not daring to look at him.

Inside, her heart sunk like a brick. She knew this was coming. She knew very well Sam couldn't stay here with her forever. It had only been a few days and yet, she'd gotten so used to him being there, it felt as if it *could* go on forever.

She felt Sam staring at her, then he turned in his seat and looked straight ahead. "It's the only place we can agree on so far. Still, I have to admit I'm feeling pressured." He shook his head and took a sip of coffee. "I guess the only way to figure it out is to get back there and see the place one more time. It wouldn't be fair to my partner if I don't even talk it out with him face-to-face."

"No, that wouldn't be fair." She waited, wondering if he would say anything about them. About their relationship.

"If you have any problems with the lease, call me. Maybe I can help," Julia offered.

He smiled at her slowly. "Okay, I will. I'm probably going to call you every hour on the hour, just to hear your sexy voice. Of course, that's going to be pure torture, since I won't be able to touch you again, at least until the weekend."

He was going to come back on the weekend? That was only… Four days from now. Julia felt so relieved she could have hugged him. But she somehow restrained herself, trying to act as if she'd expected it all along.

"The weekend? That sounds…okay."

"I hope so," he teased her, moving closer to rub his cheek against her hair. "You don't have anything planned? No hot dates lined up that I should know about?"

Julia laughed. "If I did, I'd be a fool to admit it. Don't worry, I can clear my calendar," she said, teasing him back.

"Good. That's all I wanted to hear." He leaned over and kissed her deeply. "I'm going to miss you," he whispered.

"Me, too," she sighed.

"Three days isn't so long."

It is if you missed someone with all your heart and soul, and the bed was suddenly empty and cold. And your house was suddenly too quiet and your heart felt like a stone.

Julia sighed, unable to say any of those things.

"It's actually four days until the weekend," she corrected him. "But I'll be right here."

Four days. Or forty.

Sam smiled. "Good. That's just what I wanted to hear."

Sam had already packed his few belongings in a black duffel and a short time later, Julia stood kissing him goodbye at the front door. For a moment, it seemed as if he wasn't going to leave at all. Then finally, with a shuddering sigh, he pulled away, dropped one last kiss on the tip of her nose and slipped out the door.

She stood in the doorway, peeking out as he got in his SUV, then drove away.

It was a cold, dingy gray morning. The dreariest part of the winter. The weather outside seemed to match her spirits perfectly.

Julia went up to her bedroom and took a long, hot shower. She told herself that it was good in a way that Sam had to go back to the city today. Being in his company 24/7 for almost a week now had been like a wonderful dream. But all dreams come to an end. She couldn't go on like this forever. She had a life to return to. She had a business to catch up on. She had things to do and her mother still needed attention and would need even more in a few days, when she was released from the hospital.

But all of her logical arguments didn't do much to persuade her. Not really. Of course, there were always responsibilities to attend to.

But life wasn't just one long to-do list. Julia felt as if she was just starting to get it: the reason her mother seemed so flighty and carefree. So irresponsible and impulsive at times. She just had her priorities in a different order. Love and romance were at the top of the list, instead of at the bottom, where Julia knew now she had always placed them.

No wonder she'd never been able to find a good relationship.

She emerged from the shower with one towel wrapped around her head and one around her body. She started making up the bed, but suddenly felt a little light-headed. So she sat down on it instead. The towel slipped off to the floor. Julia hardly noticed. She felt a wave of dizziness and a cold sweat on her forehead.

She lay down, wondering what was wrong with her.

For one thing, she hadn't eaten since lunch yesterday. And she had drunk too much strong coffee this morning. That had to be it.

She rested a moment, then got up again and dressed in pants and a turtleneck sweater. She decided to stop by her office on her way through town before she went to the hospital today.

Any other time in her life, she would have been champing at the bit to get back to her business. But this morning, she felt different. She cared about the realty, but it just wasn't as important to her.

She left the house toting her briefcase and headed for her car. She noticed Sam's big footprints in the freshly fallen snow and stepped inside them all the way down the front path, just to feel close to him again. She had to smile at how silly she was acting.

It didn't matter. She didn't care if she'd lost all her common sense over him. Julia knew she felt different now about everything.

The days until the weekend had stretched out endlessly once Sam had left town. But they quickly filled with Julia's routines and responsibilities, and all the things she'd put aside while her mother had been so ill.

She found herself shuttling between the hospital and her office, making brief pit stops at home just to shower and eat a few bits of whatever she could find in the refrigerator.

Sam did not call her hourly, as he'd promised. But he did call often enough to prove to her cynical side that she hadn't been imagining their special connection, or the powerful feelings he'd awakened.

On Thursday night, she left the hospital earlier than usual so that she had some time at home to clean up her house before Sam arrived on Friday. She was vacuuming when she heard the phone ring and ran to pick it up.

It was Sam. She'd been waiting to hear from him and greeted him warmly. He didn't sound quite as happy on the other end and she wondered if anything was wrong.

"You sound a little tired," she said. "Is everything okay?"

"Mitchell and I are having some problems," he said, talking about his partner. "We still haven't signed the lease and now he insists on having some restaurant designer take a look at the place before we do anything more. I think it's basically fine as it is. I don't think we have the funds for some fancy designer…."

Sam sounded mad now. Just about as angry and frustrated as she'd ever heard him. She wasn't sure what to say.

"Maybe when Mitchell gets the plans and sees how much it will cost to redecorate, he'll see your point."

"I'm hoping it works out that way, too. The problem is, this decorator is only able to meet with us on Saturday. And I definitely have to be here."

"Of course you do," she agreed. "It's important."

Important enough to stay in Boston for the weekend and miss visiting her, she realized. But she tried not to sound downcast or whiny and complaining. He'd been so understanding of her when Lucy was sick, it was her chance to show him she could be the same.

"It means I have to stay in the city," he said.

"Yes, I realize that. But this is important. I understand."

"Can you come here?" he asked suddenly. "I know the office is open on the weekend, but maybe you can shift your appointments around or something? Give some to Anita? You could help me a lot. I'd value your opinion. And I miss you madly," he added.

Julia was touched by the invitation and the tone of his voice.

He sounded so desperate to see her. The same way she felt about him. "I'd love to come, Sam. I'd love to see the place you chose. But my mother is getting out of the hospital on Saturday."

"Oh…I didn't hear the good news. Yes, of course you need to stay and help her."

His voice was subdued, and even sad, she thought. Her heart melted. "Maybe I could get away during the week. I could just come for a quick visit. If you're not too busy," she added.

"That would be great." He sounded encouraged. "Or I could get back to Vermont somehow. If I can figure things out with Mitchell."

Julia had a feeling that if it wasn't one problem with Sam's partner, it would be another. But she didn't want to sound negative.

They talked for a while longer about Lucy and Lester. Each time Julia had visited this week, she'd found the senior lovebirds busily planning their wedding and honeymoon. The pastime proved to be the perfect tonic for Lucy, who had improved quickly, and was kicking her infection in record time.

Her doctor said she was ready to go home. She needed some help in the house for a while and then would start physical therapy. Lester had already figured everything out, hired a home health aide and set up the therapy appointments.

"Your dad is very efficient," Julia told Sam. "I didn't have to make a single call or even interview anyone. He even stopped by her house one day and cleaned out the fridge, too. I can't keep up with him," she admitted.

The truth was, she'd felt a little outpaced by Lester. He was taking over Lucy's care, which was a burden off Julia, it was true. But it left a gaping hole in her life and she could hear a lonely wind blowing through.

"I don't mean to sound ungrateful," she told Sam. "He's been wonderful to my mother. But I guess I just feel…pushed aside or something. Like she doesn't need me anymore."

"Julia…honey. Don't be silly," Sam consoled her. "Lucy adores you. It's not just because you do things for her," he reminded her. "She loves you because you're you. And she still needs you…. I need you, too," he added softly.

"I need you, Sam," she answered impulsively. And she knew it was true. She felt it with all her heart.

She couldn't even remember the last time she'd said that to someone. Had she ever? she wondered.

When she and Sam finally hung up, Julia felt a wistful sort of melancholy. She shut out the light on her night table and rolled to her side, hugging a pillow to her chest. A tear squeezed out of the corner of her eye and rolled down her cheek.

Opening her heart to Sam had changed her life. But now she was feeling the flip side of caring for someone, the difficult part that sooner or later comes. She knew she would see him one way or another. If not this weekend, then very soon after.

Yet it was painful to care this much. It scared her to realize that—not this time, but some time—it could all be taken away.


When the weekend arrived, Julia focused on Lucy. Working with Lester, they had made Lucy's house clean and inviting, with fresh flowers in every room from all the bouquets friends had sent to the hospital. Lucy was very pleased to be home again and kept thanking them both profusely for everything they'd done.

Eleanor Weeks stopped by and dropped off a casserole. She sat and visited with Lucy and traded gossip from the card-playing club. Lucy was back in fine form, Julia noticed, the color rising in her cheeks as she gathered juicy tidbits of neighborhood news. It was hard to guess what she'd gone through the past few weeks.

Except that she did tire easily. Lester had her chatting sessions on a kitchen timer. When the buzzer went off, he made her hang up the phone, or bid her guests goodbye.

Julia loved the system but knew if she had tried it, her mother would have taken the timer and tossed it out the window.

Lucy was still on a restricted diet, but on Sunday night while they all watched TV together, Lester insisted on going out for ice cream. "Come one, let's celebrate a little. You can have a little ice cream, Lucy."

"I would like some," she admitted. "Maybe a small hot fudge sundae?"

A hot fudge sundae was not the healthiest choice for a woman with clogged arteries. But Julia held her tongue. She didn't want to be a spoilsport and with all her mother had survived, a small ice cream sundae seemed a tiny thing to ask.

"Julia, what can I get for you? Same as your mom?" Lester asked.

"How about just a single scoop in a cup? I'm sort of on a diet." Her clothes had been pinching lately. Too much of Sam's good cooking, no doubt. Still, she couldn't resist a little cup of ice cream. "Maybe something with…coconut in it?"

Not her usual choice. But she was feeling adventurous lately and had this odd craving for coconut all weekend. She'd even bought herself a package of macaroons in the grocery store. It was…strange.

"Coconut ice cream?" Lucy laughed. "I ate that by the gallon when I was expecting you. It was hard to find. There was only one dairy way out in Westfield that made it. I'd make your father drive there, day and night."

Julia had often heard that story. But tonight it made a new impression on her. She'd been expecting her monthly cycle for a few days now and not even getting her usual symptoms. She'd always been regular as clockwork. She didn't dare allow herself to think what it all might mean.

Her body was having a reaction of some sort, she reasoned. The stress of her mother being sick. And all the lovemaking with Sam. If that didn't affect a woman's hormones, what would?

No, she wasn't pregnant just because she felt like eating some coconut ice cream. Julia nearly laughed out loud.

Leave it to her mother to plant some ridiculous idea like that her head.

* * *

A few days later, Julia wasn't laughing anymore. Her period was still missing in action. Late one night on the Internet, she'd searched women's health topics and found that her body was blossoming with all the classic signs of…pregnancy.

On Wednesday she left the office early and went straight home with a bag full of pregnancy detection kits. She tried them all and each version gave the same answer.

The dot turned blue. The line turned pink. The sensor sounded. What more proof did she need?

Julia didn't know whether to jump for joy, or shriek in sheer horror.

She was going to have a baby.

Sam's baby. There was no question about that.

She had always been so careful about protection. How had this happened? Sam had been very thoughtful and careful about it, too. But there were a few impulsive moments when they'd been in such a rush. Or just feeling so relaxed they'd forgotten all about it.

It had happened entirely by accident.

But there is no such thing as an accident, she argued with herself. Sigmund Freud didn't think so. Especially when it came to getting pregnant. Her rational side just wouldn't buy it.

You wanted a baby and so you managed to trick Sam into making one with you. Without even asking him. Isn't that right, Julia?

She sighed. It wasn't like that. Not at all.

For goodness' sake, she hadn't made herself pregnant. He knew what he was doing. He wasn't entirely blameless in the situation.

Julia flopped back on her bed and released a giant sigh. "Watch what you wish for." The simple nugget of greeting card philosophy echoed in her brain.

Now there were words worth tattooing on her forehead.

The phone rang. She turned her head on the pillow and heard the machine pick up, then listened for the caller.

It was Sam. Of course. She'd been expecting his call.

She hadn't been able to get to Boston this week and he hadn't been able to get back to Vermont, even for a day. He was going to let her know tonight if he'd be back this weekend.

She had been thinking about him all day, practically counting the hours until Friday night, when he might be with her again.

Now she felt terrified of seeing him and her mind raced with excuses of putting off the visit.

She felt awful lying there, listening to him talk to dead air. But she couldn't help it.

She couldn't pick up the phone and speak to him right now. Maybe not even later tonight.

This news changed everything.

## *Chapter Ten*

When Rachel arrived at her store the next morning at half past eight, Julia was already there, waiting at the door, sipping a cup of herbal tea.

"Julia? Is everything all right? Is something wrong with Lucy?"

"Lucy's fine. Everything else in my entire life is a huge, unbelievable mess. And it's all my fault besides…" she ranted quietly.

Rachel rested a gentle hand on her shoulder as she opened the shop door.

"Come on in. Let's sit down and talk." Rachel gently guided Julia into the shop. Once they were comfortable in two seats at the front counter, Rachel turned to her, ready to listen.

"This is about, Sam. Right? Are you upset that he hasn't come back to see you yet?"

Julia sighed. "At first I was. I mean, I just miss him. We talk every night and I know that he's not avoiding me. He left a message last night that he's coming back this weekend. But now…I feel like leaving town. I just can't face him…."

Julia swallowed hard. Rachel was staring at her, looking totally confused. "I don't get it. Did you meet someone else you like better?"

"Oh, no…nothing like that." Was there a man alive on the planet that she'd ever like better than Sam? Julia knew it wasn't possible.

She took a breath and folded her hands around her paper cup, which was filled with caffeine-free tea instead of her usual mega dose of black coffee.

"Rachel…I'm pregnant."

There, she'd said it out loud to someone. Julia waited for the earth to stop spinning on its axis. She waited for the sky to fall. She held her breath and glanced at Rachel, wondering at her reaction.

"Are you sure? Maybe you're just late."

"I bought a truckload of pregnancy kits—I cleaned out an entire shelf in Drug Mart—and I did them all last night. They all turned out positive." She took a breath. "And I have all the other classic textbook symptoms. Including a craving for anything with coconut…which is not a classic symptom, I know. But it seems to be hereditary."

She glanced down at her muffin, not her usual whole wheat and cranberry but something called Morning In Paradise, loaded with golden raisins and chunks of toasted coconut shreds.

Rachel smiled gleefully, then leaned over and gave Julia a tight hug. "I'm so happy for you! It's all worked out perfectly."

"I would hardly call the situation perfect, Ray." Julia stared at her.

"Sam doesn't know yet," Rachel said. "But he's coming this weekend, you can tell him then."

"I'm not so sure about that. I mean, telling him." Julia felt a familiar wave of panic wash over her again. "It's not as if we have any sort of commitment. He's never said a word about the future. And I have no idea how he feels about children. He might hate the idea of having a baby. But if I tell him, he'll feel obligated to me. I know the way he is. That's not what I want at all."

Rachel gave Julia a long, thoughtful look. She reached across the counter and patted her hand. "I understand what you're saying, but…I have to be honest with you. I think he has a right to know, Julia. He's the baby's father…and with Lucy and Lester getting married, you can't avoid him. You might be able to disguise your pregnancy since he's living so far away. But once the baby comes…well, you can't hide a baby."

Julia had thought about all that. She'd stayed up all hours of the night, the different scenarios twisting through her tired brain.

"I thought about all that. I've been thinking this might be a good time to move away. My mother is very happy with Lester. I think she finally did find her *soul mate,* after all these years. She doesn't need me taking care of her anymore. I've always fantasized about living in a big city, someplace hot and sunny where the winter isn't so long and depressing. I can sell my house and my business. I'd definitely have enough money to get a good start."

Rachel frowned. Julia could tell her friend didn't like this plan at all.

"Oh, Jules, I know you could do it all on your own. Start off someplace new, raise a child by yourself. No one would ever say you couldn't. But think about it carefully. I would miss you so much. All of your friends would. Lucy would be beside herself. Even if she has Lester, she still needs you. And your baby would never get to see its grandparents," Rachel reminded her.

Julia didn't answer. She'd considered that, too.

She'd considered every possibility. But she still had no idea what to do.

She covered her face with her hands, trying not to cry.

"It's such a mess. And I'm so emotional lately. All the hormones bouncing around. That's another thing. I can't even think straight…."

Rachel patted her shoulder as Julia began to sniffle. "Sorry to tell you this, but this pregnancy business? It's going to get worse before it gets better."

"Thanks for the tip," Julia said wryly. "What am I going to do, Ray? I'm so confused."

Rachel sighed. "Honestly? I don't know what to tell you. But I know what kind of person you are. I think you'll figure out the right thing to do," she said quietly.

Julia appreciated her friends confidence but wasn't at all convinced she would live up to Rachel's expectations.

When Julia strolled into the office a short time later, Marion looked up from her desk and nearly gasped out loud.

"Geez, Julia. You look awful…."

Julia's eyes widened. "Thanks, Marion. Thanks a lot."

Her assistant colored, looking only slightly embarrassed at her frankness. "Sorry…but…do you feel okay?"

"I couldn't sleep last night." That was, in fact, true. Though not the entire reason she looked like roadkill this morning.

"Any messages?" she asked briskly, trying to get back into business-day form.

Marion handed over a pile of pink slips. Julia flipped through them as she went into her office. Sam had called. Twice. She guessed he'd also left at least one message on her cell phone, but she'd uncharacteristically kept it shut off today.

She had to call him back. She couldn't avoid it any longer. She would keep it short and simple, and try to sound as normal as possible. Brisk and distant, as if she was terribly busy in the office and didn't have time to chat.

She closed her office door and dialed his cell phone number.

He picked up on the first ring. "Hey, Sam. It's me."

"Hello, me. Good to hear your voice." She could hear the tender smile in his voice and it melted her resolve.

"I got your message last night," she continued. "I'm sorry I wasn't able to call you back."

"Were you out on the town with some other guy?" His tone was teasing but she wondered if he wasn't just a little concerned.

"Oh, you know me. I don't get out much…. I was already in bed, totally beat." That was technically not a lie, she told herself. She had been lying on her bed when he'd called.

"Well, rest up. I'm coming to see you tomorrow night. We'll have the whole weekend together."

The soft, seductive note in his voice gave no question as to what he was thinking.

"Yeah. That will be…great," she said with false cheer. "So, how is it going? Did you ever sign that lease?"

Sam sighed. She had the feeling he wasn't alone and couldn't speak freely. "There's a lot going on. I'll tell you all about when I see you. I'll lose my mind if I don't see you soon," he said sweetly.

She felt the same way, too, at times. She missed him so much. It was like an ache in her bones.

"Yes, soon," she said quietly. "Listen…I've got to run. See you tomorrow night."

She knew if she talked any longer she might break down crying and tell him everything.

Sam said goodbye and ended the call. Julia let out a long breath and sagged in her desk chair.

She had barely made it through a three-minute phone call. How was she ever going to survive an entire weekend, carrying around this enormous secret?

Julia left the office early and went over to visit her mother. It was one of the few times since her mother's return from the hospital that Julia did not find a friend or two visiting. Julia had some good friends in town, Rachel being her best. But her mother was the unofficial goodwill ambassador of Blue Lake, Vermont. She had friends of all ages, sexes, shapes and sizes. She made friends wherever she went and had lived in the town most of her life. Julia was very impressed by the sheer number of people who stopped by or sent cards or flowers, wishing Lucy well. She had to give Lucy credit. It was a rare and admirable talent.

Lucy had been home from the hospital almost a week. She was growing stronger every day but still grew tired easily and couldn't be alone for long periods of time. Lester was out doing errands and Julia found her at the dining-room table, sorting out mounds of old photographs and pasting them into scrapbooks and photo albums.

Julia had made her mother and herself some tea and brought it in from the kitchen. She served Lucy and then sat down at the table.

"I've been meaning to go through these old pictures for years. Seems like a good time since I'm stuck in the house with nothing to do." Lucy looked up at her. "And a good time to look back, since I'm making big plans for the future now."

For all her air-headed affectations, her mother did have a philosophical side, Julia reflected.

A photo caught her eye and Julia picked it up. "Mom…you dressed me in the funniest outfits sometimes. And that bow in my hair. I look like a helicopter."

Julia had to laugh at her little-girl image. It looked like a first day of school picture. She was standing at the elementary school bus stop, dressed meticulously—albeit ridiculously—and proudly holding up a new lunch box. Care Bears. Julia had adored it.

"I think you look adorable." Lucy snatched the photo away and sighed. "Take a look at this one."

She handed over an even older photo. Julia as a baby, about six months, sitting on a blanket in a sunsuit.

"Did you ever see such a cute little dumpling? You were a such a beautiful baby," her mother went on. "Everybody said I should have taken you around to the modeling agencies—"

"Thank goodness you didn't listen to them, Mom," Julia interrupted with a laugh.

"I bet when you have a baby they're going to look just like that, all dimpled with big blue eyes…."

Julia blinked. Her breath caught in her chest for a moment.

She had in fact been picturing a baby lately, but the child had brown eyes and thick dark hair.

"It will depend on who the father is, too, don't you think…? I mean, who knows about these things. I may never even have a baby," she added nervously.

Lucy looked up at her. "Oh, I have a feeling about that." She nodded. "You know when I was lying there so sick in the hospital, I said to myself, 'You can't check out now, Lucy, you're never going to get to see your grandchildren.' I knew if I died, that was the one thing I'd regret the most."

Julia had to smile. Her mother's confession was very touching…and amusing at the same time.

"Mom, if someone is deceased one would assume they would no longer be burdened with regrets."

Lucy laughed. "Oh, I get it. Sure. But you know what I mean." She leaned closer and rested her hand on Julia's arm. Julia could still see the purplish bruises where her mother had worn an IV, reminding her again how close she'd come to losing Lucy just a short time ago.

"Julia, I know I seem like a ditz to you at times. But I'm a bit sharper than you think, dear. I've had my eye on you lately, young lady." She nodded sagely, using an expression Julia had not heard since high school. "Now tell me the truth. Are you pregnant?"

Julia's head snapped back. How in the world had her mother guessed?

"Mom…don't be silly. What gave you that idea? Just because of that ice cream the other night?"

Lucy shook her head. Julia could see she wasn't going to be put off so easily. "I have eyes in my head. The way you've been acting. The mood swings…"

"Mood swings? I don't have any mood swings," Julia insisted, at the same time, feeling her eyes fill with tears.

She groped through her pocket for a tissue and pretended she needed to blow her nose.

"And you look pretty dreadful, I must say. No offense," her mother added in a concerned tone.

"Gee…thanks, Mom."

"Well, if your own mother can't be honest with you about these things, who can?"

"My secretary?"

She knew the quip wouldn't make any sense to Lucy, but it felt as if everyone had been on her case today. She had to vent.

Lucy sighed and gave Julia a wistful look. "I promise I won't tell a soul. Not even Lester. And I don't need to know any of the details…though I'd bet my retirement accounts I could guess who the father is…." she added in a little singsong tone.

Julia sat with her arms crossed over her chest, her lips pressed together in a tight line.

"Julia…please? After all I've been through? Knocking on death's door, dear? I just want to know if I'm going to be a grandma. Is that too much to ask?"

Julia felt her stoic stance dissolving. Her mother always knew how to get her way, just what to say to push Julia's guilt buttons. But Julia still wouldn't say. She looked at her mother, then looked away.

"You'll start showing sooner or later. It's hard to keep this type of thing a secret for very long," Lucy reminded her.

Julia finally turned to her. "Mom, listen to me closely. I'm only going to say this once. I am not expecting a baby. I've been working hard, trying to catch up at the office and I'm probably coming down with a cold or something," she added.

Lucy looked surprised. She leaned closer. "Are you sure?"

"Of course I'm sure. What a question. Wouldn't I know such a thing?"

Lucy shrugged. "Not necessarily…"

Julia shook her head. "I'm sorry if you had your hopes up. You're just going to have to wait."

Not as long as you might think, either, she wanted to add.

But she couldn't tell her mother the truth yet. Her mother could never keep a secret if her life depended on it.

And she didn't need an entirely new problem to worry about, Lucy broadcasting the news to the entire free world.

*Then I really would have to run off and hide in some remote spot,* Julia thought. *I wonder how the day care is on Tierra Del Fuego.*

Julia lived in dread for the next twenty-four hours. She couldn't eat a thing except weak tea and saltine crackers. She wondered if it was round-the-clock morning sickness setting in, or just nervous anticipation over seeing Sam again.

It hardly mattered. The sum effect was the same. She felt exhausted but couldn't sleep. Her house looked perfect, like a picture in a magazine. But she looked like the "before" photo in a makeover show.

She waited for Sam in the spotless living room, wearing a black velvet jogging suit—the very one he'd practically ripped off her body the first time they'd made love, she recalled regretfully. Her hair was pulled back in a tight ponytail and she felt too tired and defeated to even put on earrings, or try to cover the purple circles under her eyes with some cover stick.

*The worse I look, the easier this will be,* she told herself.

If he decided to just scoop her up and make love to her, she wasn't sure she could handle it. She had a plan and she hoped she could stick to it.

Sam appeared on her doorstep at a few minutes past nine. Julia had seen the SUV pull into the drive and was already at the front door.

His broad, warm smile undid her completely. Without saying a word he pulled her into his arms and lifted her completely off her feet.

"Julia. I missed you so much." He pressed his cheek to hers. His skin was cold from the outdoors, and she breathed in the heady scent of him, his familiar cologne and soap—it was a distinctly male smell.

"Sam…oh…let me down. Please?" She struggled for a moment to get free of his embrace. He stared at her, totally bewildered as she raced for the guest bathroom just off the foyer.

"Julia, are you all right?"

"I'll be right out," she managed to shout through the closed door. Then she got sick. As quietly as possible.

She splashed her face with cold water and dabbed at her eyes. You are not going to cry. Get me? she told her image in a fierce inner voice. Not until this over and he's out of here.

She pulled up the zipper of her hoody a notch, so as not to encourage any distractions. Then she stepped out of the bathroom and returned to the living room, where Sam sat waiting for her, perched on an armchair.

He looked worried. "What's wrong? Are you sick?"

She waved her hand in the air. "I seem to have caught some kind of bug. It was going around the office."

"Oh…that's too bad. Well, we can just stay in this weekend. I don't mind. We can rent some movies. I can take care of you, Julia."

She glanced at him, then looked away. Where would she ever find another guy like Sam? But she couldn't think of any other solution.

"Listen…we need to talk," she said suddenly. She looked up at him and could tell her manner and tone had snared his attention.

He had the "Uh-oh…relationship discussion" look on his face that men got all the time. He leaned back in his chair and opened up his jacket.

"Sure. What did you want to talk about…? Did I do something wrong?" he asked innocently.

Julia rose from her seat on the couch. She paced the floor in front of him. "It's not you, Sam, honestly. I think it's just me. This just isn't working for me, this long-distance relationship thing." She glanced his way, to gauge his reaction. He looked surprised, but not angry. Not yet, anyway.

"It's just too hard for me. And you're so busy with your new business and I'm busy, too…and let's face it. We're very different. I mean, we had some wonderful times together. But I've been thinking and…I don't think this would work out in the long run. Why put ourselves through a lot of unnecessary grief?"

Now he looked totally shocked. And angry. He stood up and faced her. "What are you trying to say, Julia? You don't want to see me anymore?"

"Sam…please…" Julia pressed her hand to her head. She didn't want to hurt him. She never thought he'd react this way. So…hurt. It pained her, too, to go through this charade. But she felt she had no other choice. She just didn't want him to know she was pregnant with his baby.

If he stayed the night, she was sure she'd end up telling him everything. And regretting it.

"It's all for the best, believe me. I think some difficult circumstances drew us together. Which was understandable. But…I don't think this could ever last. We're just too different."

His dark brows drew together in an angry frown. "Did you meet someone else? Some lawyer or banker or something? You have some cookie-cutter idea about the kind of man who would be best for you and I guess I just don't meet the standards, is that it?"

He was nearly shouting now and Julia didn't answer.

"Except in bed, of course," he added before she could even think of what to say. "I guess you found me acceptable when you needed some attention and sympathy…and some good sex. But now that the crisis is over with Lucy, you don't want me hanging around anymore. That's it, isn't it?"

Julia shook her head. She felt as if she was going to cry and couldn't stop herself. She felt shocked and misunderstood.

"That's not it at all," she shouted back at him.

He stared at her, his dark eyes full of pain and disappointment.

She would have done anything at that moment to have him look at her again the way he had the moment he'd come through the door.

She had the urge to just tell him everything. That she was simply crazy about him, and had never felt this way about anyone. But she was afraid. Afraid of her feelings for him and afraid now that he didn't feel the same way.

Even if she told him all that now, he probably wouldn't believe her. He'd suspect she was just trying to manipulate him again.

She definitely couldn't tell him now that she was pregnant with his child. Then he'd really feel used.

"Save it, Julia. I heard this little speech once before. Remember? After the first night we spent together. You ran scared. And like an idiot, I came after you." He met her gaze and held it. "Well, I'm not going to play that game again. I promise you. This is absolutely it."

"That was different…you don't understand," she shouted back, then had to stop herself. This time was different, but she couldn't explain why.

Sam glanced at her, then stalked over to the front door and grabbed up the duffel bag he'd dropped there only a few minutes before.

"You know what your trouble is? Sometimes you're just too practical. You always want to play the sure bet, instead of the long shot. But you'll never win big that way. Believe me."

His words stung. Mostly because she knew that his unflattering assessment was true.

She stepped toward him. She didn't want him to leave this way, so angry and cold. She'd made a mess of this conversation. She'd never imagined he'd get so…emotional. She never imagined she would get so emotional.

She never guessed it would matter this much to him.

That was a good sign, she realized. But too little, too late.

"Sam, please. Don't go like this," she said quietly.

He stopped for a moment, but didn't turn around to look at her. She waited, breathlessly.

Then watched him step out the door and slam it shut behind him.

Julia stood perfectly still. She could hear her own heartbeat, the blood pounding through her veins. She felt light-headed, having lost just about everything she'd tried to eat for the last few days. She knew if she fainted, Sam wouldn't be there to catch her this time. So she held on, squeezing her eyes tight, listening.

After a moment, she heard his SUV start up with a roar and she knew he was gone.

She felt her cheeks wet with tears. Then she ran into the bathroom and got sick again.

The next morning, Julia felt dreadful. She felt like staying in bed all weekend but forced herself to get up and get herself into the office. It was Saturday in late February. She really didn't need to be there. But she knew she couldn't stand to hang around her empty house, rehashing her goodbye argument with Sam.

Marion was in and seemed surprised to see Julia. "Oh...I didn't expect you. Isn't Sam in town this weekend?"

Was her private life an open book to the entire world? Julia fumed.

Julia ignored her question. "Any messages, Marion?"

Marion handed over one slip. "Just your mother."

Julia stared at the message a moment, wondering if Sam had just turned around and gone back to Boston, or stayed to visit with Lester. Whatever Lester knew, Lucy would know, too. She had to expect that.

Even if Sam was still around, if she stayed in her office and went straight home, she'd be very unlikely to see him. Then he'd go back to Boston and that would be that.

It was all for the best, she told herself for the umpteenth time. Sam had been angry at her but had also hit a few painful bull's-eyes. She *was* overly practical at times and was hung up on as-surances. For example, she'd needed some assurance that he really cared for her. That his outraged reaction wasn't just a mat-ter of his pride being hurt.

If he did really care for her, he would have said so, wouldn't he? Not just walked out without a word. But he'd never even mentioned it. So…maybe it was best if she just let him go. He had his life in the city, a new restaurant opening, all the pretty girls who would work there and or dine there and flirt with him night and day….

Her imagination started to run away with her and Julia strug-gled to get a grip.

Well, he'd soon forget all about her. She was sure of it.

Even when her mother and Lester got married, how much would she see him? Not very often. Besides, she really could move away. It wasn't just a silly fantasy. She'd always wanted to leave this place. Here was the perfect opportunity.

It would be difficult. But she could do it. She could move far away and manage to avoid him completely. No one would ever know he was the father of her baby. Except Rachel, of course. And she wouldn't tell…would she?

Julia's mind spun in crazy circles. But the dark image of Sam—sad, disappointed and hurt—was always front and center.

On Saturday the office usually closed around four, unless one of the salespeople was trying to reel in a buyer. But the day had been quiet, with few calls and even fewer customers. It was the lull before the rush in the spring when all new listings came on the market.

Even Anita had gone on vacation to Cancún. Now that was saying something, Julia realized, passing by her top sales-woman's empty desk as she headed back from the copy machine.

Everyone was gone for the day but Julia remained, trying to clear every last paper and miscellaneous file off her desk. Just busywork, but she needed to keep busy. She wasn't sure how long she'd force herself to stay here. Until she felt just about exhausted but not too tired to drive herself home and fall into bed?

The phone rang. She heard the machine pick up. She expected a client, asking about an ad from the newspaper. But she heard her mother's voice. Then she realized she'd forgotten to return Lucy's call.

Julia strained to hear her message but couldn't quite make it out since the machine was outside on Marion's desk. She would play it back later when she left. Then she would call her mom tonight from home. Julia felt too tired to talk to anyone at that moment and even simple conversations with Lucy could be a challenge.

She sat back in her chair. Who was she kidding? She hadn't slept well for a few nights now. She had to go home and get some rest. Maybe now that she'd had her confrontation with Sam, she could actually fall asleep.

She doubted it. His sad expression would haunt her all night long. But she had to try. Getting overtired like this could not be good for the baby. She touched her flat stomach with her hand. Hard to believe, but there was another life growing in there and, God willing, she was going to be a mother at last. All her wishing and hoping and daydreams were finally coming true. Just not in the way she had imagined.

But beggars could not be choosers, and she had to keep focused on the silver lining in this mess. No matter how badly she felt about losing Sam, she was going to have a baby—his baby—and that was absolutely the most wonderful thing that had ever happened to her.

With her spirits a notch higher, Julia pulled on her coat, grabbed her purse and began shutting off the office lights, preparing to lock up. She was just about to leave when she saw someone at the door, cupping his hands around his eyes and peering inside.

It was Sam. Before she could do anything about it, he opened the unlocked door and walked in.

"You shouldn't leave the door unlocked like this when you're all alone in here at night, Julia. It's not safe," he said mildly.

"I was just leaving." She stepped back. There was something in his overly calm manner that alarmed her. Or maybe it was just the shock of seeing him here, when she hadn't expected him. And the fact that it was so dim and shadowy, with only the light from the streetlamps illuminating the room.

He wore a long black wool overcoat and a black sweater underneath. He looked very big and…threatening.

"I thought you must have gone back to Boston by now." She struggled for an even tone, hardly the way she really felt.

"That would have been convenient for you. I meant to," he added quietly. "But I stayed in town to visit my father. I told him what happened. That we decided not see each other anymore," he added. "Or rather, you decided for us."

Julia felt her heart start to pound. She wasn't sure why, but the very tone of this conversation was beginning to feel very ominous. As if somewhere in the background a time bomb was slowly ticking.

"What did he think of that?"

"He felt sorry for us. Sorry for me, actually," Sam clarified.

He sat on the edge of a desk and tilted his head to one side, looking down at her. The room was dark and shadowy, she could hardly see his face. But she felt stuck in place, unable to even reach for a light switch.

"Your mother had an interesting take on it."

"My mother?" Julia felt truly alarmed. "My mother was there?"

"I had to go to Lucy's house to see my dad. He hardly leaves her side since she's been ill."

Julia knew that. What had she been thinking? Lester and Lucy were a package deal now.

"Your mother says you're having a baby, Julia. My baby. Is that true?"

His words were sharp, slicing through the darkness and Julia's carefully rehearsed pretenses.

"I never told her that," Julia insisted.

"She told me you'd deny it. She said you denied it when she asked you, but she's positive it's true. Motherly intuition, I guess. But you'll be learning all about that pretty soon, won't you?"

Julia sighed. She sat down heavily in an desk chair. She could stand here and argue with him all night. But now that he'd caught the trail, he wouldn't be put off. It was no use. She had to tell him. The game was up.

She looked up at him, then nodded. "I am having a baby. It's true."

Then she braced herself, as if she were suddenly seated in the midst of stage-five hurricane.

She had a feeling that the angry blast she'd felt last night was nothing in comparison to what was to come.

"My baby?"

"Yes," she said quietly.

"And when were you going to tell me this, Julia?"

Julia sighed and shrugged. "I—I don't know. I didn't know how to tell you, Sam. I know how you are. I don't want you to feel obligated."

He stepped back, and his eyes widened. She thought for a moment he might laugh at her. Then his expression was deadly serious again.

"Your mother said you were thinking of going to a sperm bank to get pregnant. But this was much better. At least you know who the father is and it didn't cost a cent. Those places can be quite expensive, I hear."

Julia felt herself grow beet-red. How dare her mother tell Sam all that! This was simply unbearable.

She jumped up and faced him. "That's not true. I guess I did mention it once to her. In passing. It's not as if I'd ever done anything about it. I do want a baby. Like most women my age…"

"So you don't deny it. You wanted a baby and you met me and it seemed to all fit into your plan. How practical, Julia. I saved you some time, money and worries, too. Your mother was concerned about the sperm donor plan. She said you could have gotten pregnant from a crazy man. It was much safer the way it worked out with me. She thinks anyway," he added drily.

"There was no secret plan," she argued through gritted teeth. "You're the one who's being crazy now, Sam."

"Am I really? You used me, Julia. Admit it. I was a total push-over, too. Mr. Free Sperm Bank. Is that what you think of me?"

Julia took a deep breath. He was over-the-top now. Someone had to get a grip and bring the conversation down to a reasonable level.

"Sam…just stop talking a minute and listen to me. I can see why you might come to all these wild conclusions after talking to my mother. But that wasn't the way it happened at all. It was an accident. We used protection," she reminded him. "Except for maybe once. Or twice? When we got carried away. And you can't say this is entirely my doing," she pointed out. "I mean, you were definitely there. You have to take some responsibility."

He didn't answer for a long moment. Julia wondered what he was thinking. He looked thoughtful. Subdued. She hoped her quiet words had brought him around to a more reasonable attitude.

"I do take responsibility," he said finally. "Absolutely. This is my baby, too. And I want the child to grow up with two parents. In a real family. I want us to get married."

His proposal shocked her, though, in fact, she had expected him to react this way. But it was different hearing the words spoken out loud.

"I didn't set out to trap you, Sam, if that's what you think," she said. "To trick you into making me pregnant and then trap you into marriage."

He crossed his arms over his chest. "I never said that. Well, not the last part. I think it was just the opposite. I think you thought you were going to take the sperm and the baby and run. Well, that's not going to happen, Julia. I promise you. The best thing for us to do is take a page from your book and be practical about it. Babies need two parents. It's the reasonable thing to do."

He was turning her tactics against her. Very clever.

But Julia wasn't even mildly persuaded. For once, being practical and reasonable had no appeal for her whatsoever.

"It would never work," she said flatly. "Just because I'm having your baby doesn't mean we have to get involved in some ill-advised marriage that's bound to fail. You forget. I've seen my mother get married too many times for the wrong reasons. I'm not about to follow in her footsteps."

"I think this is a good reason. One of the best," he argued quietly. "I can barely think of a better one."

How about being in love? she nearly snapped back at him. She thought that was a good one.

In fact, the real reason she'd flat-out refused his proposal was just that. He'd never once mentioned being in love with her. He'd never even hinted he was even slightly in love with her.

Oh, they were good in bed together. He'd reminded her of that often enough. But that wasn't love. She knew the difference and so did he. He was just like every other man after all, wasn't he?

Maybe she was not the most romantic woman in the world. Maybe she hadn't been looking for true love all these long years of being alone. But something had changed for her and now she understood what all the commotion was about. Why people wrote about, sang about it, were willing to toss themselves over a cliff for it.

She finally got it. And she knew she couldn't settle for less. Not unless Sam felt the same. And he obviously didn't, or he would have said so.

He was the only man, she realized now, who had ever truly stolen her heart. Tonight, arguing with him here, she suddenly had no doubt. She was deeply, madly and impossibly in love with him.

Just her luck.

"So, that's your answer? You won't marry me? You won't even consider it?" His harsh tone cut through her wandering thoughts. "I understand. I was good enough to get you pregnant. But not to marry."

"Sam, that's not fair."

"Don't tell me about fair. You're having my child and you didn't even plan to tell me. Was that fair? Or honest? I had to come here and—and…interrogate you."

She did feel as if had done exactly that, sitting in the darkened office, looking so big and ominous in his long dark coat.

"Well…now you know," she said simply.

She felt suddenly angry all over again. She was tired of this exhausting argument. Tired of being accused by him of femme fatale schemes that had never in a million years crossed her mind.

Tired of loving him and not even being able to touch him.

It was all suddenly just too much.

She picked up her purse and slung the strap over her shoulder. "I'm locking up now. You have to go," she said briskly.

She looked at him squarely, summoning every shred of energy and willpower to hold on and not back down. Not cry and melt into a puddle of apologies.

He looked surprised but stood up and faced her.

So far, so good, she thought.

It was like facing down an alpha dog, she realized. If she didn't put up a cold, hard front now, she'd never get through this in a million years.

"This isn't the end, Julia. You're not getting rid of me this easily," he warned her.

His threatening tone did make her worry. What was he planning? Lawyers? Custody agreements? Dragging her through a legal maze of paternity rights?

She didn't say anything. She walked to the door and opened it. "Good night, Sam," she said simply. "Goodbye."

He stared at her angrily, then stalked to the door with giant steps. He stood directly in front of her a moment, staring down into her eyes.

She tried very hard to look away. But she couldn't. His head dipped toward her and she was mesmerized, her gaze wandering from his eyes to his lips.

She wondered for a moment if—after all—he was about to kiss her.

Then he suddenly turned away and swept through the open door, quickly disappearing down the dark street.

A cold wind blew into the office. It rattled the plate glass window and stirred up loose papers like a tiny tornado.

An omen of things to come, Julia thought.

And not a very comforting one.

## Chapter Eleven

Lucy apologized profusely. She claimed she had never meant to give Julia's secret away, but had just been thinking out loud, trying to make some sense of why Julia would toss aside "a perfectly lovely hunk of a man" like Sam.

"Lester and I just couldn't understand it. I was just taking a wild guess. And I told Sam you had totally denied it," she added. "I started off talking about hormones and how they can make a woman lose her head sometimes. Especially when she's expecting…. And then, well…one thing led to another, I suppose. And you never even said you were. You denied it. I told him that…."

Julia found it totally ironic, too, that she had purposely not confided in her mother, but Lucy ended up giving away her secret anyway.

Some things were meant to be. Like Sam finding out the truth about their baby. Julia wasn't even mad at her mother. Not really. She knew now she'd been fooling herself to think she could keep the truth from him for very long. In a way, it was a relief that he knew.

And an even greater relief that he'd gone back to Boston. There was no telling when he would return. Maybe not until Lester and Lucy's wedding, which was now planned for the middle of April, a little more than a month away.

Julia visited her doctor, who said that everything was coming along just fine, all healthy and normal. She didn't need to return for another exam for a few weeks.

She left the office with armloads of pamphlets covering all phases of maternity, from diet and exercise to maternity yoga and the possible benefits of playing classical music next to the mother's belly.

She sat in bed at night, surrounded by the pamphlets and piles of books, some that she'd found in the bookshop in town and many that Rachel had given her. Many intimidatingly thick. And there was even more information on the Internet. She doubted that her mother—or many women in her mother's generation for that matter—had felt the need to immerse themselves in this encyclopedia of pregnancy knowledge. They just got pregnant... and had a baby.

She had a feeling that if Sam had been sitting there beside her, he would have been making fun of her studying up so diligently. She imagined how he would take care of her and their baby, feeding her nutritious gourmet meals. Making sure she got to bed on time. Picking out names from the baby books with her. Sometimes she could almost hear his voice, or imagine him close to her. Especially when she turned out the light.

He was never far from her thoughts, day or night. His parting words echoed through her mind. "You think you've gotten rid of me but this isn't over, Julia." Over two weeks had passed since he'd cornered her in her office that dark night. She had fully expected by now to find a letter in the mail one morning, on official-looking legal stationery, demanding all Sam's parental rights and then some.

But day after day, there was no word from him. Or an attorney. Julia wasn't sure if that was a good sign or a bad one. Part of her felt as if she'd been left dangling on a string waiting there, until she dropped.

Even Lester and Lucy never mentioned him anymore and Julia was too proud to ask. They invited her over for dinner regularly and at each visit Julia could see that her mother continued to recover from her surgery, until Julia realized that if she didn't know Lucy had ever been so seriously ill, she would have never guessed it.

Lucy was back to all her former activities, including card parties next door, Jazzercise classes and serious shopping trips. The baby had opened up a whole territory to explore at the outlet mall and Lucy seemed determined to conquer it.

Sitting in the living room after dinner one night, Lucy pulled out her latest finds for the baby, including clothes, toys and all kinds of things to decorate the room. "Mom, really. You're totally overdoing it. You've bought enough stuff for three babies and I'm not even done with my first trimester."

"I've been waiting years for this, Julia. I think you're just going to have to grin and bear it. We can always save the extra things for future babies."

Future babies? Julia thought the chances of that were slim to none. She felt struck by lightning just to have this one.

"Speaking of the future," Lester said, "we've decided to change our plans, Julia. We thought you should know. We're not going ahead with the goat farm idea after all. I don't think it would be wise, considering Lucy's health." He looked sad, Julia noticed. But resigned. She was secretly happy to hear the news, but also realized Lester was giving up a lifelong dream and that had to be hard.

"But we've reached a nice compromise," Lucy added. "Tell her, dear," she coaxed Lester.

He slowly smiled. "Well, Lucy had this idea of opening a store in town instead. A cheese shop, where we could sell fancy cheeses and crackers and maybe even some wine and kitchen gadgets. I can make cheese on my own in a nice shop. I don't really need the goats," he added.

"I have a little experience working in retail. At Rachel's store," Lucy reminded Julia. "Rachel said I was a very good sales-woman," Lucy boasted.

Julia did remember that now. Rachel had needed some help in the shop right after she'd opened up and Lucy had worked there part-time whenever Rachel had a busy season. All Julia could remember was how her mother started such long involved conversations with the customers, she ended up hearing everyone's life story. And telling her own.

But that was probably a good thing in a small town. Julia thought that between Lester's and Lucy's various talents, they'd do very well with their own business.

"I think that's a great idea. There aren't any shops like that in town right now and the tourist trade is really picking up around here in the fall. It's a nice compromise," she added, glancing at Lester.

"Talking things through. Compromise. That's the key to a successful relationship," Lester said, slipping his arm around Lucy's shoulder.

Julia wondered if he was thinking more about her and Sam, and how they couldn't talk anything through or compromise. She pushed the thought aside and tried to change the subject.

"There are a few empty shops in town for rent right now. I'll check the listings for you," she offered. "Maybe we can get appointments and take a look this weekend."

"That would be a big help. Thank you, Julia—" Lester began.

"But we'll be busy this weekend, dear," Lucy finished for him. She sat up straight in her chair, smiling widely. She looked at Lester and he smiled, too.

"We have something else to tell you," Lester said slowly.

"We're going to get married. At a justice of the peace up in

Bar Harbor. Now that I'm feeling back to my old self, we just didn't want to wait any longer," Lucy explained.

This was a surprise. But Julia tried to improve on her reputation for being bad with surprises. She could see that Lester and Lucy were nervous, waiting for her response.

"I think that's just…terrific. Bar Harbor is a beautiful place to get married," she added.

"We're still planning on a big party with family and friends," Lucy said happily. "Sometime in the spring. Maybe after we open the store."

"After all Lucy's been through, we decided we just wanted a quiet, private little ceremony. Just us two for now. We hope you understand, Julia," Lester said with concern.

"I understand. It's just what I would do, too," she assured him.

She knew that the older couple had been through a great deal the last few weeks and had a perfect right to forgo all the wedding hoopla. But she also had the feeling this change in plans was partly due to the trouble between herself and Sam. They had both been asked to be in the wedding party, as best man and maid of honor. Lucy and Lester probably didn't know what to do and dreaded bringing their children together for their happy day, as if inviting a pile of dynamite and blowtorch to come up on the altar with them.

Julia realized she'd be sorry not to see her mother and Lester exchange vows, but was also deeply relieved she'd been let off the hook so easily.

When would she next see Sam now? She had no idea.

The worst of the winter was over, Julia decided. She strolled up Main Street on Monday morning, after visiting Rachel at her shop. The trees were still bare and patches of snow dotted the sidewalk. But the light breeze that lifted her hair felt milder, the sun seemed brighter and felt warmer on her skin.

The weather definitely lifted her spirits and Julia felt cheerful as she crossed Main Street and headed for the realty office. But when she reached the corner, she noticed a familiar figure about halfway down the street. Archie Newland, her local business rival. He was peering into a storefront window, a café that had been empty and available for rent for months now.

The exclusive listing of Home Sweet Home Realty. All of her salespeople had shown it, but so far there hadn't been any takers. Now that spring was coming, Julia expected some smart entrepreneur to snap it up. The property was in a prime location and visible to everyone going in and out of town.

Did Archie think he was going to steal the listing from her now, after she and her staff had put their time in?

No way, buster, Julia silently fumed.

She marched across the street, and tapped him on the shoulder. He jumped and turned, then offered her an automatic, and embarrassed, smile.

"Julia…I was just coming to see you," he improvised. "I may be able to move this one for you. If you want to make a deal on the commission. I was showing a client some of my own listings, but he got interested in this one. You know how fickle they can be. Always want the one they can't get…."

Julia crossed her arms over her chest and gave him a tight smile. "Nice try, Archie. I think your client needs to get inside before they decide to rent it. Too bad I have the only set of keys and the owner is down in Florida."

Archie sighed. "Be reasonable. It's been a slow month all around town, Julia. I'm not asking for the whole pie here. Just a taste. Unless you have another tenant lined up? One with excellent credit, able to move fast on a long lease, option to buy?"

The client did sound like a good catch. Why hadn't they come to her agency? The sign in the café window was very bold and clear—Home Sweet Home Realty.

"How did you find this exemplary tenant?"

"I found Mr. Newland," a deeper voice answered. "Seems he's the only *other* game in town."

They both turned to face Sam, who had walked down the alleyway from the back of the building, checking out what he could through the dirty windows.

Julia took a long moment to check him out.

Handsome as ever, maybe even more so, with the light breeze ruffling his thick hair and the collar on his leather jacket snapped up to his chin.

She felt a giant sigh building at the sight of him but didn't dare release it.

"Hello, Sam. Real estate shopping?" Julia said quietly. "I told your father I'd find a nice shop for him. You didn't have to come all the way from Boston to do it."

"I have no idea what you're talking about, Julia." Sam cast her a puzzled look. "I'm looking for a spot to open a restaurant...."

Archie had been following their conversation, turning his head from side to side, as if watching a tennis match. He cleared his throat suddenly and Julia realized she'd been totally oblivious to him once Sam had filled her field of vision.

"I gather you two are acquainted. How nice," Archie said quickly. "I have to run to another appointment now. I'll catch up with you later, Julia. We'll talk, okay?"

"Yes, we'll talk, Archie," she promised.

She turned back to Sam, still unable to totally process that he was standing right in front of her. Looking for a place to start a restaurant. What this some sort of trick to wheedle his way back into her life?

"Excuse me if I'm having trouble getting up to speed here," she said.

"That's okay. We haven't been in touch for a while, Julia. Life goes on. Things change, you know?"

His tone was cold, distant. Was he trying to tell her that he was over her? On to something new? Someone new? That's why he was able to come back here?

"What happened to the place in the city?" she persisted. "The one you were going to redecorate?"

"That didn't work out. Mitchell backed out of our partnership. Which is just as well. Our ideas were not in synch. It left me free to start something of my own. Which is what I've always wanted to do. I can afford to be independent out here."

He crossed his arms over his chest and stared down at her.

"So...you're definitely relocating?"

"That's right. Frankly, I didn't like the idea of being so far away from the baby. So it works out all around. I'm not going to be one of these phantom fathers, Julia. I can promise you that. You know I'm a hands-on kind of guy."

Julia felt her stomach fall. She did know that. But tried not to reminisce too much.

"I gather this place is your listing," he said, glancing at the sign in the window. "Are you going to let me in?"

"Sure. Why not?" She turned. "Come across to my office. I'll get the key...and have someone help you."

Did he think they were going to work together on this rental idea? All the calls back and forth. All the visits and driving around town, looking at properties.

Think again, pal. It's not going to be that easy.

Sam followed her into the realty office, his hands jammed in his coat pockets.

"Have a seat," Julia said, offering him one of the visitor chairs by the front door. "Someone will be with you in a minute."

Her polite, impersonal manner peeved him. She could just tell by the look on his face as he sat. *One point for my side,* she decided.

She went back to Anita and explained that she was handing off a really good client interested in the restaurant across Main Street. Anita had been having a slow week and sprang into action, like a hound dog let loose to track down her prey.

Julia brought Anita to the front of the office and introduced her to Sam. "Anita is a star around here, Sam. I know she'll take excellent care of you."

Anita's eyes widened, taking in Sam's good looks. She glanced at Julia as if to ask, "You're sure you want to let this one go?" A moment later, they were out on Main Street, Anita jangling a ring of keys in her hand, and steering Sam over to the vacant building.

Of course he had to pick something right in her sight line, Julia fumed. He couldn't even be on the other end of Main Street! Between Lester's cheese shop and Sam's restaurant, this town was getting overrun with Baxters. She was starting to feel squeezed out.

Julia tried to focus on work for the rest of the day and not think about Sam, if he was serious or just playing with her. Anita did not return until a few hours later. Julia was dying to ask what had happened, but forced herself not to interfere.

Finally, at the end of the day, Anita came to her doorway. "Julia, do you have another phone number for the man who owns that restaurant across the way? I've been trying to call all day and I just get a funny busy sound."

So Sam was interested. Julia felt her heart sink.

"I have a cell phone number. Let me look." She riffled through some papers tucked in the edge of her blotter. "So did Sam Baxter like the property?"

"Oh, yes, he said it was perfect for him. He liked the kitchen layout, too. He's not interested in renovating, wants to open up quickly." Anita met her eye. "He's a very dynamic man. Very decisive."

"Yes…I know," Julia mumbled.

What did her staff know about her relationship with him? She hadn't told anyone in the office the whole story. But she knew that they gossiped and Marion overheard all her private conversations, whether she wanted to or not.

She finally found the number and jotted it on a yellow Post-it note. "Do you think he's serious? Not just looking?"

"He's definitely serious." Anita seemed surprised by the question. "He wants a long lease and is willing to pay for it. I smell a nice deal brewing here."

Julia swallowed hard. "Good luck," she said quietly.

Her morning sickness, which had disappeared for weeks, returned that night with a vengeance. Julia was not surprised. The doctor had told her her cause of morning sickness was mysterious, but stress was definitely a factor.

It was Sam's return that had brought it back again. Julia was certain of it.

Rachel agreed. Julia had asked her over for dinner for moral support. Though she couldn't eat a bite of the tasty pasta dish she'd prepared, Rachel seemed to enjoy it.

"Now I'm doomed to spend the next eight months feeling miserable and sick. And afraid to stray too far from the nearest bathroom," she vented to Rachel. "All because of him. Why did he have to come back…and plant himself in my town? It's just not fair."

Her friend listened patiently, lending Julia a sympathetic smile. "I think this latest development is very interesting. I don't doubt his story. It's sounds like he's well rid of that difficult business partner. But I do think it's suspicious that he chose this town for his new business. Right across the street from your office. I think he's had some time alone and he wants to make up with you, Julia."

Julia wished that was so. But she'd seen the cold, distant look in his eyes. She'd felt his disinterest when there once had been a connection strong enough to light up Times Square.

"He's just not into me anymore, Rachel. I read the book. I saw all the telltale signs. He told me he's doing all this for the baby and for once, I believe him. As much as it hurts to admit it," she added.

The realization that he didn't care anymore stung and made her own feelings seem so foolish and hopeless.

Rachel didn't answer. She reached over and rubbed Julia's shoulder. "Don't worry about that now, Jules. I don't think he even knows what he's doing here. You know how men are. Act first, think later."

"Don't I ever. That's what got me into this situation in the first place." Julia sighed.

Rachel laughed. "Want some more crackers and ginger ale?"

"I'm good. I don't want to overdo it," she added with a wry smile.

"I brought along a few things for the baby. Let's take a look. Maybe that will cheer you up." Rachel reached into her big tote and pulled out a shopping bag from her store.

"Oh, Ray, please. You have to stop," Julia pleaded with her, before she even opened the bag. "Between you and my mother, I have enough stuff to open my own store."

"Don't you dare." Rachel's tone was serious, though her eyes showed only good humor.

"Seriously, I know the baby won't be here for a while, but I have to get started on the nursery. I have no place to put everything. It's getting out of hand."

"Let's go upstairs and take a look. I want to paint a mural for you," Rachel reminded her. "I want to see the space so I can get some ideas."

Wall mural painting for children's rooms was one of the decorating services Rachel offered at her store. She did all the murals herself. Rachel was so creative and an amazingly talented artist and seamstress. Julia was glad for her friend's expert advice on decorating the baby's room. She also knew the project would take her mind off of Sam. At least a little bit.

Julia didn't see Sam over the next few days, though she knew Anita was going back and forth over the phone with him and the property owner regarding details on a lease.

She guessed he was staying at Lester's house in Dorset, which was some reprieve. She wouldn't actually have to deal with him face-to-face on Main Street until he got the keys to the place. Which could take some time with the property owner still down in Florida.

All of this information didn't help her from feeling as if she was on pins and needles every time she set foot in town, expecting Sam to pop out in front of her at any moment.

If this was how she had to live the rest of her life, Julia was sure her nerves couldn't take it. She'd have to move away, just to keep her sanity.

She'd been running an open house on Friday afternoon. It was very crowded and she'd kept it open longer than advertised. When she returned to the office it was nearly six o'clock. But Sam was there, taking care of some business with Anita. He rose when she walked past and practically stood in her way so that it was hard to pass.

Julia was glad he had at least caught her at a good moment, appearance wise—they did come so few and far between these days. She'd had enough energy to blow out her hair that morning after her shower and had dressed in a smart dove-gray suit with a long jacket that hid her tiny puff of tummy.

Her body was undergoing other changes, too, besides her expanding waistline. None of her tailored blouses seem to fit well anymore and her sweaters made her look like a Victoria's Secret model. Sam seemed to notice, too. She could see the glint of male approval in his dark eyes, assessing the changes in her figure, especially as it passed over the taut fabric of her silk blouse that outlined her full breasts.

"So, how is your deal going? Did you finalize everything yet?" She kept her tone brisk and businesslike, the same she would use for another client. Or so she told herself.

"We're ready to sign on the dotted line." Sam lifted the sheaf of papers in one hand. "I'm just going to have my lawyer take one more look."

"Well…good luck."

He stared at her but didn't answer. She felt he was about to say something more personal. To cut through their polite, impersonal chatter. But then Anita appeared and interrupted.

"That copy machine always jams. Sorry for the wait." She handed Sam some forms and then left a stack on her desk.

"Well, I guess that's it. Just bring that back when you've signed and we'll send it to the owner."

Then she quickly gathered up her purse and jacket. "I've got to run. Call me if you have any more questions."

"I will," Sam said. "Thanks again."

He turned to Julia and she was very conscious that they were alone. "So…it's after six. Are you going to stay here longer?"

She tilted her head to one side. "I'm not sure. Is that really any of your business?"

"Of course it's my business. I don't want to see you working too hard. It's bad for the baby. I bet you're not eating right, either. You look…thinner." The corner of his mouth twisted down in a half smile. "Certain parts of you."

"I've had a lot of morning sickness. Not just in the mornings."

Lately because of you, she wanted to shout at him.

He looked concern. "Is that all right? I mean, can it hurt the baby?"

"It's fine for the baby. Pretty unpleasant for me, though."

He looked genuinely concerned. "I'm sorry, Julia. I didn't realize you were having such a rough time. Can I take you out to dinner? We should probably start talking…about everything."

Julia felt a frisson of alarm. Here it was. By "everything" he meant child custody arrangements. How much time he would be allowed to have with the baby and under what circumstances. The entire topic totally distressed her. Not that she didn't trust him or think he would be a caring, responsible father. She had no doubt that he would. But it was more the idea of splitting up the baby, shuttling the child back and forth between two houses, even if those houses were right in the same small town.

She just didn't like it. She just didn't want her child to go through all that.

She looked up at him, feeling suddenly angry. "I'd rather not have dinner with you, Sam. Thanks all the same. And I'm not ready to talk about…anything. Especially having to do with the baby."

His head snapped back, surprised at her strong response. For a moment he looked angry, as if he might start an argument with her again. Then he took a deep breath and his expression softened.

"All right. Maybe this is not a good time," he said diplomatically. "I'm going back to Boston for a few days to pack up some more of my things. But whenever you're ready to talk, just let me know."

She nodded, but didn't say anything. He looked deeply into her eyes a moment, then turned away and walked to the door.

He was going to Boston, to have his lawyer look over the lease…and discuss the custody terms he'd demand of her, Julia was sure of it.

In a few days, the string she'd been dangling on would finally snap.

Julia did not feel well all weekend. She decided to stay at home and rest on Saturday and Sunday. She could hardly remember the last time that had happened. But her mother's illness had taught her that the office could carry on fine without her constant hovering.

To keep herself occupied, she decided to start on the baby's room. The room was supposed to be a guest room, but Julia rarely entertained any out-of-town guests and it had become a catchall for everything she planned to give to charity or was just too lazy to carry into the attic.

Just moving the unnecessary furniture, boxes of old clothes books and all kinds of odds and ends would be an achievement. She didn't have much energy, but she hated to just sit in bed or even on the couch, and she'd read her fill of baby books.

So she pushed herself to work on the room, at a slow but steady pace. But on Saturday night, she wondered if she'd overdone it. She was too tired to even eat. Late at night in bed, she felt her stomach rumble with cramps. She braced herself for a dash to the bathroom, but was spared. Still, she didn't feel right and hoped a good night's sleep was what she needed.

Julia slept late on Sunday, then lounged around in her bathrobe, reading the newspaper. Rachel was going to stop by in the afternoon and show Julia some ideas for the mural. With the room cleaned out, Julia thought they could get a good idea of how it would look.

She fell asleep reading the paper and woke with a foggy head and stomach cramps. She ran into the bathroom, thinking she had a virus, but soon realized it wasn't that at all. Julia had read enough about pregnancy to know that something was very wrong.

She ran to the phone and dialed her doctor, but only reached the service. She quickly left a message, then hung up the phone. How long would it take for the doctor to call her back? She had no idea. Perhaps she should drive herself to the hospital. But it was far and what if she felt even worse on the way?

A knock on the door startled her and snapped her out of her runaway panic. Rachel. She'd come early. Thank God.

Julia ran to the door and pulled it open, practically panting with anxiety.

But it wasn't Rachel at all. It was Sam. He looked down at her, his expression uneasy. "I stopped by the office and they said you've been out sick the whole weekend. Are you all right?"

Julia stared at him. She felt her mouth go dry. It was so hard for her to admit that she needed some help. From him. That she needed him.

She pulled him by the arm and tugged him inside. "Something is wrong. I just called the doctor. She hasn't called back. I'm scared, Sam," she admitted, staring at him.

He gripped her by the shoulders and looked into her eyes.

"It's okay. Just tell me. What should we do?" His voice was calm and reasonable, his entire body alert.

"I think you should take me to the hospital. To the emergency room. Right away."

Sam nodded. Then he put his arms around her and pulled her close. "It's going to be all right, Julia. Don't worry."

She clung to him briefly, trying hard not to cry. Then she stepped away and grabbed her purse from the table in the foyer. Sam brought her a jacket that had been hanging on the coat tree, and she stuck her bare feet into insulated boots. She didn't care what she looked like. She just wanted to get to the hospital.

He helped her into the passenger side of his SUV, then jumped behind the wheel. Sam drove quickly. They soon reached the highway. He looked totally focused, his expression grim.

"I thought you were in Boston for the weekend," she said finally.

"I came back this morning." He glanced at her. "I just had this funny feeling that you needed my help."

Did he still feel something for her? Or was his concern only for the baby? Julia tried not to get her hopes up. She couldn't think about anything right now but her baby. Not even Sam.

He reached over and took her hand. She met his dark gaze, then looked out at the road. She knew he was just trying to comfort her, but it was still wonderful to touch him again after all the time they'd been apart.

But his comforting touch wore down her defenses. Julia felt tears welling up in her eyes. "Sam...I'm so stupid. I didn't feel well and kept working on the baby's room.... If anything happened to the baby, it's all my fault...."

"Julia...don't worry. Let's hope for the best." He put his arm around her shoulder. "Let's just wait and see what the doctor says."

Julia nodded, trying to gain control again of her emotions. His tone was comforting, but his expression was still grim, she noticed.

Julia's cell phone rang. She saw that it was her doctor and quickly answered. She explained her symptoms to Dr. Rowan and answered a few of her questions. "You've done the right thing going to the E.R., Julia. I'm on my way," Dr. Rowan said. "I should be there in about half an hour."

Julia thanked her and hung up. "That was my doctor," Julia told Sam. "She's going to meet us at the hospital."

"Good. Did she say what she thought was going on?"

"No," Julia said quietly. She didn't think that was a good sign and could see from his expression, Sam didn't think so, either.

Dr. Rowan had already arrived and was waiting for Julia in the E.R. Julia was quickly brought into an examining room. "I'm going to examine you, Julia, and then we'll need to do a sonogram to see what's going on and check on the baby. The man who brought you in…is he a friend?"

Julia sighed. "He's the baby's father."

"Would you like him to be here with you?"

Julia didn't pause a moment to consider the question. "Yes, please. Could he come in? I mean, if he wants to?"

Dr. Rowan smiled at her, pulling on her gloves. "I think he does."

The examination was quick and routine. Dr. Rowan didn't say much one way or the other. Julia was moved over to the sonogram machine and the nurse prepared her for the test, rubbing cold gel over her belly.

The lights were dim and Sam walked in. He rushed to her side and took her hand, then put his face close to her own and gently kissed her forehead. "How are you doing? Are you okay?"

She gazed up at his handsome face, the face she'd come to know and love so much. She felt teary-eyed again. "Oh, Sam… I'm so sorry. Can you ever forgive me?"

He hushed her and softly kissed her lips. "Forgive you? I love you, Julia. I love you so much. Don't say those things. It's not your fault. The doctor will tell you that. I want the baby, too, but if this pregnancy doesn't work out, I still want to marry you. We'll try again. We can have all the kids you want, I promise."

Julia felt her heart lift, despite the heavy weight of worry. "I love you, too," she murmured. "Probably from the first minute I saw you," she admitted. *Even though I was too stubborn and close minded to realize what had happened.*

Sam kissed her deeply and she kissed him back with all her heart and soul. He loved her. He really did. Whatever happened, they'd get through it together. And stay together. Forever.

They heard the doctor reenter the room. "I'm ready to start now. If you could just step back a bit, Mr. Baxter?"

Sam shifted, still close to Julia and holding her hand very tight. The doctor ran the sensor over Julia's abdomen and watched the small black-and-white screen.

"I see the baby," she announced. Then she paused.

Julia couldn't breathe. She squeezed her eyes shut. The moment of silence dragged on, feeling like an hour.

Finally the doctor said, "The baby looks fine. Everything seems to be on track. No problems." She looked up at Julia. "It's just as I thought. You have a low-lying placenta. That's what caused the bleeding and cramps. You need to stay off your feet for a while. No work. No strenuous activity around the house, either."

Julia felt so thrilled and relieved she couldn't speak.

Sam leaned over and hugged her tight. When he pulled back she could see his expression was beaming but there were tears in his eyes, too. "Don't worry, Doctor. Leave it to me. I'll take care of her," he promised.

Julia just smiled. She touched his cheek with her hand.

She had found "the one"—her true love, her soul mate. The man she didn't even think existed. Now she believed in all the romantic and sentimental exaggerations she'd once dismissed as silly fantasy and wishful thinking.

It wasn't fantasy. It was real.

As real as Sam's kiss and the strong grip of his hand holding her own.

"Sam, if the baby is a girl, I know what I want to name her," she said suddenly.

He looked at her curiously.

"Lucy. After my mother." Julia slowly smiled. "I think I owe her one."

Sam laughed. "She brought us together.... So do I."

He leaned over and kissed her deeply, holding her as if he'd never let her go and Julia knew her new life—impulsive, romantic and even impractical at times—had just begun.

* * * * *

**THOROUGHBRED LEGACY**
*The stakes are high when it comes to love,*
*horse racing, family secrets*
*and broken promises.*

*A new exciting Harlequin continuity series coming soon!*
*Led by* New York Times *bestselling author Elizabeth Bevarly*
*FLIRTING WITH TROUBLE*

*Here's a preview!*

THE DOOR CLOSED behind them, throwing them into darkness and leaving them utterly alone. And the next thing Daniel knew, he heard himself saying, "Marnie, I'm sorry about the way things turned out in Del Mar."

She said nothing at first, only strode across the room and stared out the window beside him. Although he couldn't see her well in the darkness—he still hadn't switched on a light...but then, neither had she—he imagined her expression was a little preoccupied, a little anxious, a little confused.

Finally, very softly, she said, "Are you?"

He nodded, then, worried she wouldn't be able to see the gesture, added, "Yeah. I am. I should have said goodbye to you."

"Yes, you should have."

Actually, he thought, there were a lot of things he should have done in Del Mar. He'd had *a lot* riding on the Pacific Classic, and even more on his entry, Little Joe, but after meeting Marnie, the Pacific Classic had been the last thing on Daniel's mind. His loss at Del Mar had pretty much ended his career before it had even begun, and he'd had to start all over again, re-building from nothing.

He simply had not then and did not now have room in his life for a woman as potent as Marnie Roberts. He was a horseman first and foremost. From the time he was a schoolboy, he'd known what he wanted to do with his life—be the best possible trainer he could be.

He had to make sure Marnie understood—and he understood, too—why things had ended the way they had eight years ago. He just wished he could find the words to do that. Hell, he wished he could find the *thoughts* to do that.

"You made me forget things, Marnie, things that I really needed to remember. And that scared the hell out of me. Little Joe should have won the Classic. He was by far the best horse entered in that race. But I didn't give him the attention he needed and deserved that week, because all I could think about was you. Hell, when I woke up that morning all I wanted to do was lie there and look at you, and then wake you up and make love to you again. If I hadn't left when I did—the way I did—I might still be lying there in that bed with you, thinking about nothing else."

"And would that be so terrible?" she asked.

"Of course not," he told her. "But that wasn't why I was in Del Mar," he repeated. "I was in Del Mar to win a race. That was my job. And my work was the most important thing to me."

She said nothing for a moment, only studied his face in the darkness as if looking for the answer to a very important question. Finally she asked, "And what's the most important thing to you now, Daniel?"

Wasn't the answer to that obvious? "My work," he answered automatically.

She nodded slowly. "Of course," she said softly. "That is, after all, what you do best."

Her comment, too, puzzled him. She made it sound as if being good at what he did was a bad thing.

She bit her lip thoughtfully, her eyes fixed on his, glimmering in the scant moonlight that was filtering through the window. And damned if Daniel didn't find himself wanting to pull her into his arms and kiss her. But as much as it might have felt as if no time had passed since Del Mar, there were eight years between now and then. And eight years was a long time in the best of circumstances. For Daniel and Marnie, it was virtually a lifetime.

So Daniel turned and started for the door, then halted. He couldn't just walk away and leave things as they were, unsettled. He'd done that eight years ago and regretted it.

"It *was* good to see you again, Marnie," he said softly. And since he was being honest, he added, "I hope we see each other again."

She didn't say anything in response, only stood silhouetted against the window with her arms wrapped around her in a way that made him wonder whether she was doing it because she was cold, or if she just needed something—someone—to hold on to. In either case, Daniel understood. There was an emptiness clinging to him that he suspected would be there for a long time.

\* \* \* \* \*

## THOROUGHBRED LEGACY
*coming soon wherever books are sold!*

*Thoroughbred* *Legacy*

## Launching in June 2008

### A dramatic new 12-book continuity that embodies the American Dream.

Meet the Prestons, owners of Quest Stables, a successful horse-racing and breeding empire. But the lives, loves and reputations of this hardworking family are put at risk when a breeding scandal unfolds.

*Flirting with Trouble*

### by *New York Times* bestselling author

# ELIZABETH BEVARLY

Eight years ago, publicist Marnie Roberts spent seven days of bliss with Australian horse trainer Daniel Whittleson. But just as quickly, he disappeared. Now Marnie is heading to Australia to finally confront the man she's never been able to forget.

*The stakes are high when it comes to love, horse racing, family secrets and broken promises.*

*A new exciting Harlequin continuity series coming soon!*

# REQUEST YOUR FREE BOOKS!

## 2 FREE NOVELS PLUS 2 FREE GIFTS!

# SPECIAL EDITION®

## Life, Love and Family!

**YES!** Please send me 2 FREE Silhouette Speãal Edition® novels and my 2 FREE gifts (gifts are worth about $10). After receiving them, if I don't wish to receive any more books, I can return the shipping statement marked "cancel." If I don't cancel, I will receive 6 brand-new novels every month and be billed just $4.24 per book in the U.S. or $4.99 per book in Canada, plus 25¢ shipping and handling per book and applicable taxes, if any*. That's a savings of at least 15% off the cover price! I understand that accepting the 2 free books and gifts places me under no obligation to buy anything. I can always return a shipment and cancel at any time. Even if I never buy another book from Silhouette, the two free books and gifts are mine to keep forever.

235 SDN EEYU  335 SDN EEY6

| | | |
|---|---|---|
| Name | (PLEASE PRINT) | |
| Address | | Apt. # |
| City | State/Prov. | Zip/Postal Code |

Signature (if under 18, a parent or guardian must sign)

### Mail to the **Silhouette Reader Service:**
**IN U.S.A.:** P.O. Box 1867, Buffalo, NY 14240-1867
**IN CANADA:** P.O. Box 609, Fort Erie, Ontario L2A 5X3

Not valid to current subscribers of Silhouette Speãal Edition books.

**Want to try two free books from another line?**
**Call 1-800-873-8635 or visit www.morefreebooks.com.**

* Terms and prices subject to change without notice. N.Y. residents add applicable sales tax. Canadian residents will be charged applicable provinãal taxes and GST. This offer is limited to one order per household. All orders subject to approval. Credit or debit balances in a customer's account(s) may be offset by any other outstanding balance owed by or to the customer. Please allow 4 to 6 weeks for delivery. Offer available while quantities last.

**Your Privacy:** Silhouette is committed to protecting your privacy. Our Privacy Policy is available online at www.eHarlequin.com or upon request from the Reader Service. From time to time we make our lists of customers available to reputable third parties who may have a product or service of interest to you. If you would prefer we not share your name and address, please check here. ☐

SSE08

# Romantic
# SUSPENSE

**Sparked by Danger,
Fueled by Passion.**

Seduction Summer:
Seduction in the sand...and a killer on the beach.

*Silhouette Romantic Suspense invites you to the hottest
summer yet with three connected stories from some
of our steamiest storytellers! Get ready for...*

## *Killer Temptation*
### by Nina Bruhns;
a millionaire this tempting is worth a little danger.

## *Killer Passion*
### by Sheri WhiteFeather;
an FBI profiler's forbidden passion incites a
killer's rage,

### and

## *Killer Affair*
### by Cindy Dees;
this affair with a mystery man is to die for.

**Look for**

KILLER TEMPTATION by Nina Bruhns in June 2008
KILLER PASSION by Sheri WhiteFeather in July 2008
and
KILLER AFFAIR by Cindy Dees in August 2008.

*Available wherever you buy books!*

# COMING NEXT MONTH

### #1903 A MERGER...OR MARRIAGE?—RaeAnne Thayne
*The Wilder Family*

For Anna Wilder, it was double jeopardy—not only was she back in Walnut River to negotiate a hospital takeover her family opposed, the attorney she was up against was long-ago love interest Richard Green. Would the still-tempting single dad deem Anna a turncoat beneath contempt...or would their merger talks lead to marriage vows?

### #1904 WHEN A HERO COMES ALONG—Teresa Southwick
*Men of Mercy Medical*

When nurse Kate Carpenter met helicopter pilot Joe Morgan in the E.R., their affair was short but very sweet...and it had consequences that lasted a lifetime. Kate had no illusions that Joe would help raise their son, especially when he hit a rough patch during an overseas deployment. Then her hero came along and surprised her.

### #1905 THE MAN NEXT DOOR—Gina Wilkins

Legal assistant Dani Madison had learned her lesson about men the hard way. Or so she thought. Because her irresistible new neighbor, FBI agent Teague Carson, was about to show her that playing it safe would only take her so far....

### #1906 THE SECOND-CHANCE GROOM—Crystal Green
*The Suds Club*

When the fire went out of his marriage, firefighter Travis Webb had to rescue the one-of-a-kind bond he had with his wife, Mei Chang Webb, and their daughter, Isobel, before it was too late. Renewing their vows in a very special ceremony seemed like a good first step in his race for a second chance.

### #1907 IN LOVE WITH THE BRONC RIDER—Judy Duarte
*The Texas Homecoming*

Laid up after a car crash had taken all that was dear to him, rodeo cowboy Matt Clayton was understandably surly. But maid-with-a-past Tori McKenzie wasn't having it, and took every opportunity to get the bronc rider back in the saddle...and falling for Tori in a big way!

### #1908 THE DADDY PLAN—Karen Rose Smith
*Dads in Progress*

It was a big gamble for Corrie Edwards to ask her boss, veterinarian Sam Barclay, if he'd be the sperm donor so she could have a baby. But never in her wildest dreams would she expect skeptical Sam's next move—throwing his heart in the bargain....